This n
The names,
are the work of th
Any resemblance or ac
persons, living or dead, loca
events involving them, is entirely alleged
or coincidental.

Proof read/editing by Zeldos
Cover art by Orphan Print, Hereford

BEN NEVIS and the GOLD DIGGER

Book 1.

TURKISH DELIGHT

****

26 years ago.

The Juvenile Court in the Southwark Crown Court building was in session. The judge read the papers of the case before him and looked up at the boy standing in the dock with a policeman for company.

'How old are you, Ben?' he asked, taking off his reading glasses.

'Sixteen, sir.' The boy's lawyer had told him to always address the Judge as sir. No bravado, no cheek – just respect. Then, maybe...?

'Sixteen.' The judge took a deep breath. 'Not doing very well for sixteen, are you Ben.' It was a statement.

Did it require an answer? Ben wasn't sure. 'Sir?'

'Two periods in a Young Offender Institution for car thefts, and a charge of assault remaining on your file.' The judge paused for a moment or two. 'Where is your father, Ben?'

'Wormwood Scrubs, sir.'

'And your elder brother?'

'Brixton, sir.'

'Ben, you worry me. I have read the reports from your school and from the psychiatrist and probation office. You are not a fool, Ben. Your academic achievements are very good. Your school praises you, as does the Army Cadet Force you belong to, and under normal circumstances you would undoubtedly make something of yourself and your life either in commerce or the military.' Another pause. 'But coming from the family that you do, the temptation to take another path – that of criminality – is a very strong one. So what do I do, Ben? Do I send you away into a six-foot square cell for a month or two in the hope you mend your ways?'

Ben didn't answer, but the reality of the situation was beginning to break in his mind.

The judge beckoned the lawyer and the prosecutor to his bench and they spoke in hushed tones. Ben cast a sideways glance to the public gallery. The usual rubberneckers where there; some came every day, having nothing better to do – some even brought sandwiches. He locked eyes with his mother; she looked sad, and that made him feel bad. She had tried to steer him away from the family's criminal trait, but it was difficult. It felt good to have things his mates didn't have: the top of the range BMX, the latest games consoles and the latest games, an uncle with a box at the Arsenal, and most of all the attention of the local girls. It hadn't struck him that none of that would be there in a six-foot cell.

The lawyer and prosecutor went back to their desks. Ben's lawyer gave him a smile.

The judge thought for a while and then addressed Ben. 'I am given to understand that your mother has asked for total parental control, and I am minded to give you one last chance, Ben. And I mean that – this is your last chance to knuckle down and make something of yourself. You will be required to accept a curfew – that means that you must be at home between the hours of six in the evening and seven in the morning. You will sign in at school on every school day and sign out when you leave, but these restrictions will be eased at weekends. But listen to me, Ben – your mother has underwritten these conditions. If you break them, she will be in very serious trouble. Do you understand?'

'Yes sir.'

'Good. The current charge will stay on the file and if you break the conditions it will be pressed forward. You may go, Ben.'

'Thank you, sir.'

'One more thing, Ben.'

'Sir?'

'I never want to see you in this courtroom again, understand?'

'Yes sir.'

Mum had already got plans for me. Three weeks later I was having a medical for the Army, got accepted, and was on my way into a career that would end up with me being a killer! Not sure that was what the judge had in mind.

****

CHAPTER 1.
PRESENT DAY

I felt like I had wandered into the pages of an Ed McBain novel. The lady sitting in the chair the other side of my office desk was very attractive – very, *very* attractive. She knew she was very attractive too; she kept crossing and uncrossing her legs – good legs, long slim legs. Her smile was a wide smile that had no doubt launched a thousand flutters in male hearts. Mid-thirties, slim, poised, with dark hair in a forties-style bob, and her tight two-piece suit shouted money and power as much as the Gucci handbag hanging on her shoulder. The accent was Mediterranean and the slightly dark skin put her firmly in that area.

'It's not much of an office, Mr Nevis, pretty minimal,' she noted as she cast her blue eyes around.

She was right too, but who needs an expensive office when you're hardly ever there? I've got a top floor two-room office plus WC in a modern block in the Borough High Street, London Bridge end. I'd paid extra for a double parking space in the underground car park - one for me, and one for the Gold Digger. But more of the Gold Digger later. The furniture in the office is bespoke – that's the modern word for unsold ex-auction lots from the local saleroom, off loaded cheap to make room for the next lot. It had been remarked more than once that coming into my office was a bit like going back in time to the fifties. It suits me.

'I don't spend a lot of my time in here,' I countered the lady's remark whilst picking up the business card she had put in front of me when she had entered, unannounced and without an appointment. 'So what can I do for you... Eve Rambart?'

'I would like you to find my husband. I will pay you a million pounds.'

'You will, a million pounds?' Was she for real? Seeing that my usual timeframe for finding a missing person is about four days, it sounded a good deal – a ridiculously good deal. Ten years in the N14 branch of the SAS, and another ten in the Met's Organised Crime Squad when I got too old for N14 had built me a good range of contacts in both; and as most of the information on people that a private eye needs is on one or other of those organisations' databases, I could usually find whatever I needed pretty quickly. So, for a million quid this sounded a *very* good deal.

'Yes, I would like you to find him and then kill him.'

Now that didn't sound so good a deal. Okay, yes, I had killed people in the line of duty, and since I left the services and had gone private a couple more – usually a gangland hit for a mobster who didn't want it traced back to him. I do a good job, the body is never found – no body means no trail and no evidence. That's the sort of care I take. You can pay a lot less for a couple of Glaswegian knobheads on scooters with two rented pistols, but there's no guarantee of a clean kill and there's always a mess for the police to clear up that's full of clues. Rented guns are okay, but once one falls into the hands of the police and forensics analyse it against their data on bullets recovered from various killings and woundings the walls can come tumbling down pretty quickly if the renter gets pulled in and sees a plea deal as a better option than life inside and starts to talk about his clients. My current rate for a hit is one hundred grand, and the only people who know I carry out that service are very few and far between indeed. Was this lady for real? Was somebody playing a game, a joke? Her name wasn't ringing any bells in my head. If it was a gangland hit she was proposing then she was probably representing somebody else; and with so many Eastern European gangsters setting up bases in the UK recently it was quite possible and after all I thought I'd detected an accent to her voice. She was smiling at me – expecting what, to be thrown out or an immediate acceptance of the job?

'I'm not a hit man, Mrs Rambart. I'm a private detective.' I used the honorific *Mrs* as you couldn't not notice the wedding ring with a diamond big enough to plays bowls with on her left-hand finger.

'I know exactly what you are, Mr Nevis. If I wasn't confident that this sort of work was within your...' she searched for the right word, '…portfolio, I wouldn't be here. You come highly recommended.'

'I do? Who by?'

'Jameson Reynolds.'

That was a surprise. Jameson Reynolds was indeed a client of mine, and a very good one at that: an ex-gangster who had taken his ill-gotten gains and used them to progress into being a city financier and hedge fund director, operating in stocks and shares and international money movement. It's quite common for a lot of the big boys in crime to try and legitimise their businesses in the field of commerce; few succeed, but Reynolds has. I handle his security and do monthly bug sweeps of his trading floor and offices in the city. He is paranoid that his competitors are spying on him, trying to find out his money trades on Forex or what stocks he's buying and then piggyback on them. At least that's what he tells me, but personally I think he's terrified of one of his old adversaries from his criminal days taking him out with a hidden bomb – otherwise why would he insist we sweep for bugs *and* explosives? The team I hire to do the sweeps have never found a bug in six years, but now and again I take one into his office and tell him we found it. Well on a retainer of five grand a month, wouldn't you?

So anyway, I digress... Jameson Reynolds knows this lady, does he? I wonder in what capacity he knows her? She read my thoughts.

'No, we are not having an affair, Mr Nevis. Jameson is my financial investment advisor.' Her smile turned into a small laugh. 'I like the older man, Mr Nevis, but Jameson isn't my type. And nor are you,' she added as an afterthought.

I smiled back. 'I never mix my social life with my business life,' I countered, not sure whether to take umbrage that at forty-two she looked on me as an *'older man'*.

She rose and slung the Gucci over her shoulder. 'I will expect to hear from you in forty-eight hours if you will take the job, no contact if you won't.' She turned to leave and stopped at my office door, pointing to the rather discoloured lettering that had once been pristine and bright. 'Is that really your name, *Ben Nevis?'*

How many times had I been asked that, eh? 'Yes, it really is.'

'You are named after a mountain?'

'No, I am named after a race horse. My surname is Nevis, my father had an interest in a business owned by a racehorse owner and got a tip to back a horse called Ben Nevis in the 1980 Grand National and won a fortune. He celebrated by naming me Ben.'

She gave me a last smile. 'I'll expect a call.' And she was gone, leaving behind a whiff of perfume in the air that probably cost more per bottle than my monthly rent.

I studied her business card: not much information there, just the name Eve Rambart and a mobile number.

A million pounds is a lot of money for a hit, and also a lot of time in prison if you get caught. I wouldn't get caught – I work to a plan, a plan I always stick to. I've done some pretty illegal things in my time, all PIs do. Well, not all – some just do the usual *'follow the wife and see who's shagging her'* type work for divorce lawyers. Not my scene. I mainly offer protection work for celebs, keeping the fans and paparazzi at arm's length, or I negotiate with some heavy crime boss for the return of a stolen piece of art on behalf of the insurance company. They'd rather pay a thief a couple of hundred thousand pounds to get it returned than a couple of million to the policy holder if it isn't.

But I'd never been offered a hit in such an open way. With crime bosses it usually comes from an intermediary of an intermediary of an intermediary, ten steps down the ladder from the boss who orders it so he can go to the funeral and shed crocodile tears as he plots to take over the deceased's turf. I rang the Gold Digger.

Alison Gold, nickname Gold Digger – I just call her Gold: five foot eight, late thirties, medium build, hair in a fringe to her neck – sometimes she's blonde, sometimes brunette, sometimes red head – with natural brown eyes that would change depending on what colour contact lenses she had in. Overall, Alison is a nice attractive-looking lady, but beneath the well-groomed exterior lays another Alison – the Alison who's parents and siblings had been killed in their Ashkelad home by a rocket fired across the Palestinian border from Gaza into Israel by Hamas; the Alison who had refused to be fostered and formed a bad habit back in her teens of Gold Digging, hitting on wealthy men of a certain age and relieving them not of their sexual urges but of a good proportion of their wealth in cash or expensive gifts in order to live, which is where her nickname came from. She always targeted a married man with a reputation to lose or a 'celeb name', so calling in the police once you'd been duped by the Gold Digger wasn't an option if you wanted to maintain your reputation or fan base; and especially not if the duped one had a wife who might not be very understanding to the situation. Alison had been conscripted into national service with the Israeli Defence Force and found she liked the life. It gave her security and the chance of revenge for her family loss. She was soon noticed as a bit special and moved into Mossad. She was an ideal fit, exactly what they and most elite military squads want, a person with no family ties and the ability to make a cool and measured assessment of a situation. That's Alison.

We go back to the Afghan war when the N14 unit I was attached to in 2011 went into Pakistan by Chinook to cover a USA special ops SEAL unit that been sent in to kill Osama Bin Laden and then had one of their choppers malfunction. Our emergency brief was to blow up the trapped chopper if it couldn't get back and totally destroy Bin Laden's compound – anything of use to an enemy had to be destroyed.

We were low on manpower at that time with many operations against Al Qaeda going on and requested help from Mossad to assist in case the Pakistanis got wind of the operation and came to stop it. The Mossad unit we got was their Kidon unit which specialises in assassinations. Originally formed by Golda Meir in 1972 after the Munich Olympic's Israeli athlete murders to track and kill every one of the PLO Black September group that had carried out those murders. By 1979 that mission had been accomplished and Kidon was reassigned to assassinate Iran nuclear scientists and top military generals of the Iran Revolutionary Guard; the latest one being Mohsen Fakhrizadeh, their top nuclear scientist killed by a machine gun mounted on a truck and operated via a satellite using facial recognition software. It's a long way from a bullet in the head or a slit throat which were the kill options of choice in my active days.

Anyway, everything went fine at the Bin Laden compound, the USA copter got off the ground and we all fled over the Pakistan border before they could react. At the debriefings Gold and I, as heads of our units, were debriefed together to make sure our stories matched, and then we went our separate ways. I went over the age limit for N14 and was seconded into the Met's Organised Crime Squad, did a stint there and then moved into the private sector where I am now. Gold ended her association with Kidon as they only use you for three years, and went back to her elite Israeli military group Flotilla 13; finding that didn't set the adrenalin alight after Kidon, she left and went into personal security in London with a nice sideline by resuming her *gold-digging*. She made one mistake: she targeted one of my top clients, and I quickly sussed her out and stepped in. We recognised each other and became good friends and sort of business partners; she had skills in the cyber world of IT and the dark web, whilst I could present a pretty hard face to any of her victims who got nasty. As a reliable back-up, she's second to none – I wouldn't want anybody else.

'Yeah,' she answered my call – her mobile would show me as the caller. She was a lady of few words.

'You busy?'

'Waiting for a mark.'

'I'm going to text you a name to do some digging on.'

'Okay, why?'

'She's offered me a job.'

'Take it. Rent to pay, food to buy – take it. How much?'

'A million.'

'A million pounds?'

'Yes.'

'Who is the victim?'

'Her husband. How do you know it's a hit job?'

'A million quid? Bit over the top for a marital bust up, isn't it? Bit over the top for a hit too.'

'I thought that.'

She laughed. 'Tell me more.'

'Nothing more to tell. Do some digging and come round the office tomorrow afternoon and I'll fill in the gaps.'

I texted Eve Rambart's name to Gold and shut the phone. You never know who's got a tap on your phone, so I never say more than I need to. When I'm on a job I use burners and dump them pretty regularly – costs me a fortune, but keeps me safe from hackers. The society and showbiz page journos of the tabloids and internet entertainment websites know I'm the number one call for celebs and high-flyers who stray over the line and need things kept quiet and covered up, so I'd be their top target for a phone hack. And despite the *News of The World* court cases, don't think that has changed a thing – it hasn't.

****

'What have you found out?'

Gold sat opposite me at my desk the next day. I'd spent the morning smuggling a wealthy client's dipstick son out of a rehab clinic by the back door and driving him home to their Weybridge Mansion – second time I'd done it for this kid, and no doubt in my mind that the first offer he got of a coke tab would roll him off the wagon and back into his dealer's arms. It always did. I told my client a couple of heavies paying a visit to the boy's dealer would have the problem solved at half the cost of a month's rehab fee – at least it would solve the problem until another dealer tried his luck, which he would. County lines have an inexhaustible supply of care home kids willing to get out of the system with the money they can make dealing in towns and cities where their faces aren't known.

'Eve Rambart is trouble, Ben.' Gold shot me a look that said *'stay away from this one'*. 'She's on her third husband, Nicholas Rambart. Numbers one and two had accidents – lethal accidents. Number one went over the edge whilst skiing in France and fell four hundred feet down a ravine; number two had a stomach full of whisky and fell from a balcony twenty storeys up in Barcelona. Eve was with them at the time, although on both days she had alibis that placed her far enough away from the actual scene so as not to be noted as a suspect.'

'Perhaps she hired people to do the deed for her. Maybe that's what she's wanting to do with us. Local police raise any suspicions?'

'No, local courts and coroner gave accidental death verdicts in both cases. She did rather well though, both husbands were rich – honest riches. Businessmen with seats on various top company Boards and major share holders in all of them; both were in the Forbes top earners list. It all went to Eve each time. She's a multi-millionaire Ben. What's she doing hiring a hit man?'

'I don't know – with that money I would think she'd hire a lawyer to get rid of a husband.'

'Lawyers cost more than hiring you. Perhaps she's trying to do it on the cheap?' Gold laughed.

'What's her background?'

'Sketchy. She seems to have arrived on the elite social scene out of the blue. No family history of money – in fact, no family history at all. One minute she's nowhere to be seen, and then within a year she's at all the big social affairs with husband number one and becomes a paparazzi target.'

'Why?'

Gold laughed. 'You saw her, Ben. Is a paper going to pay a paparazzi more for some washed up minor reality show celeb getting out of a cab at a night club showing her knickers or Eve Rambart in a Stella McCartney one off and half of Cartier's window display draped around her neck and wrists?'

She was right of course.

'Okay, you keep on her tail. I take it you found out where she lives?'

'Knightsbridge, she's got a rental apartment over one of the shops. Expensive.'

'You think she knocks off her husbands for the money? Do you think that's what she's after this time?'

'Could be, two husbands having accidental deaths are just about believable – but three? I think that might raise a few flags with the law, so she might be looking for this one to be *murdered by person or persons unknown*. Or, she might be setting you up.'

'Setting me up?'

'You do the hit and she points the finger at you, takes the heat off any investigation into her and the two previous.'

I could see the sense in Gold's answer. 'Okay, keep an eye on her Knightsbridge place, see who comes and goes. I'll see what I can find out about the husband.'

'Before we kill him?'
'Maybe.'

****

CHAPTER 2

'I've not known her long, six months at best. Bit of a stunner, eh?'

I looked in my rear view mirror at Jameson Reynolds who was in the back of the hired Jaguar that I'd rented to take him to Heathrow. He was off on one of his many overseas trips and always insisted I did the chauffeur bit. I'd told him about my visit from Eve Rambart and that she had told me he recommended her. I hadn't told him what she wanted me to do.

'What does she do?' I asked.

'No idea. Her old man, Nicholas, is into finance and props up Middle Eastern regimes for oil and mineral rights, or used to – I think the Chinese have elbowed him out of that now. Last I heard he'd moved into arms and defence procurement, big money. I think they met somewhere in the Middle East. I've met him a few times when I went legit and put a couple of companies on the AIM listing; he was an initial buyer of their shares.' He laughed sarcastically. 'Like most things in the financial world Ben it's all a con. The bank that handles new company share issues gets a few wealthy individuals and hedge funds to underwrite the issue; means the shares are all sold and creates an interest on the Stock Exchange floor, all smoke and mirrors stuff. You can have a crap company and if all the shares are sold on the day of issue then it creates a demand and they go up. Then shits like Nicholas Rambart sell their holding and pocket a good profit. What does she want you to do, kill him?'

I checked in the mirror. He was smiling.

'Kill him?' I said with a bit of false laughter thrown in. Did Reynolds know? Had she told him?

'Well, her last two husbands popped their clogs in unusual ways and it wouldn't surprise me if she had something to do with it – she came out of both with a good bundle of dosh. To be honest Ben, I wouldn't touch her with a barge pole but she wanted a private eye so obviously I recommended you. What does she want you for?'

'No idea, said she was just checking me out and might have some work for me,' I lied.

Reynolds nodded. 'Probably some security work. I told her you handle all that sort of stuff for me.'

I dropped Reynolds off at Terminal One and gave Gold a call. I wanted to find out a lot more about Eve Rambart.

'Yeah?'

'Anything happening?'

'No, she's been across from the apartment to Harrods for some lunch and now she's back inside. Had a visit from a couple of blokes, they stayed about twenty minutes and left. Definitely Eastern European – they made a drop.'

'A drop?'

'They went in with a large holdall and came out without it.'

'Drugs?'

'Could be. I got a couple of photos through the front windows, I'll ping them over.'

'The front windows?'

'Yeah.'

'Her apartment's above a shop, how did you do that?' I couldn't imagine Gold putting up a ladder in the middle of Knightsbridge and popping up with a camera.

'There's a building of small offices opposite. One on the first floor is vacant and empty.'

'And you broke in.'

'Well, didn't take much – old Yale single lock, gives a good view into her apartment.'

I thought for a moment.

'Okay, might be a good idea to have a nosy round that apartment. I'll meet you at the front of Harrods at seven.'

****

Back in my office I took a look at the photos Gold pinged over to me. You couldn't tell much about the pair that went into the building with the holdall. A few of the photos Gold had taken through the windows with a telephoto lens showed them with Rambart in the apartment, with the time code on the snaps only moving a few minutes. It was obviously a quick business meet, not a social affair, and then they were out minus the holdall and gone. But at least Gold had got a couple of good face shots as they left.

****

It was quite dark by seven; the street lights and the car lights lit up Knightsbridge. Gold walked past me with a Burberry shoulder bag clasped to her side: our tool kit was inside. I was stood on the corner by the Harrods entrance and gave her a slight nod and followed at a discreet distance. She stopped opposite Rambart's apartment and let herself into a street door set beside a shop, leaving it ajar for me. I followed closing it behind me and hearing the lock snap across. It was dark inside and Gold shone a torch down from the first floor landing where she stood to show me the stairs that wound up around an old lift shaft that still used an old-fashioned gated steel lift. The vacant office was a one room affair, quite big with the front large picture window giving a good view of Knightsbridge below and the shops and apartments opposite. The shops were closed but the restaurants were open offering their mix of oriental and eastern foods, and about half the apartments above them were lit; I could see people moving around in some of them.

'Hers is the one over the leather goods shop,' said Gold. 'She's out by the look of it, no lights on.'

'Good.'

'The entrance door is the one on the left of the shop. I had a quick look earlier and it's a simple lever lock. I suppose they keep it simple because there's two more floors above hers, and everybody needs a key. Have you got a card?'

'Yes.' I showed her the firm but flexible plastic card the size of a credit card that I had in my pocket. 'And these,' I showed my lock picks.

'Okay. I'll keep watch, you stay listening,' She pulled a small receiver pack from her shoulder bag and an earpiece on a cord. I clipped the pack to my belt, put the earpiece in and ran the cord down under my black sweater from the neck and plugged it into the pack. She did the same with a similar pack and put on a headphone and microphone that she plugged in.

'Hear me?'

'Yes, loud and clear.' I'd be able to hear her but couldn't talk back.

'Good, here...' She handed me a pair of night vision glasses, a pair of black leather gloves and a black balaclava. 'Off you go, she might be back anytime.'

I nodded and put the night vision glasses on to make my way down the dark stairs to the front door. I took them off, put on the balaclava and rolled it up to look like a beanie hat and left the building trying to look as inconspicuous as possible as I dodged through the busy traffic crossing the road to the leather goods shop and stood like a tourist looking in the lit window. The pavement was crowded, tourists and people out for a meal moved slowly along drinking in the ambience that a busy central London can give out. I love it. Home sweet home.

'Testing, one two three,' Gold's voice came through my earpiece. 'Right arm raise.'

I raised my right arm.

'Good. All is quiet in the apartment.'

I felt in my pocket for my plastic card and walking up to the door pushed it in level with the Yale keyhole. It hit the bar and a little effort in the push slid it open and I was in, closing the door silently behind me.

'That looked easy.'

It was very dark inside, I put my night visions on; there was a switch for lights in the hallway and on the stairs but I ignored it and slipped on my gloves, pulling the balaclava down until the eye sockets were in place. I stood silently still for thirty seconds listening, just in case anybody was about on the staircase. Silence. Making my way up to the first floor and Rambart's door, I kept to the side of the stairs and listened after every two steps. The landing was clear.

Her door was more of a problem than the entrance one and took a couple of minutes with the picks before I was able to push it slowly open. I was half expecting an alarm to scream out but if there was one it was a silent one, the kind that send a signal direct to a security firm who would alert the police. In the short hallway I couldn't see an alarm keypad, so with a bit of luck there wasn't one. I moved through into the lounge that had the big windows looking out over Knightsbridge.

'I have you in view,' was the message from Gold. *'I can see you in the light from the street.'*

I checked around for a desk that might have paperwork that could tell me what Rambart was involved in. There wasn't one. I walked back through the lounge into the hallway and into the one bedroom; everything was tidy and in its place. Quickly I checked through the wardrobe and bedside cupboard – nothing that you wouldn't expect. Her taste in clothes was expensive, designer labels on everything.

That only left the kitchen-come-breakfast room, which was small and windowless off the back of the lounge so I could turn the light on without it being seen by anybody looking up from the street, anybody like Eve Rambart coming back home. I didn't have to do a search of the cupboards – a black holdall sat on the pine table. I pulled the zip along and looked inside, expecting bricks of cocaine; but no bricks were there – just guns, or to be precise Walther PPKs, six round automatic pistols packed neatly in their boxes plus twenty boxes of bullets to fit them. I remembered Jameson Reynolds had said Rambart's husband had moved into arms dealing; perhaps these were for him, or perhaps Eve Rambart was branching out on her own?

'You've got company.' Gold's warning was unemotional. I don't think I've ever heard her sound any other way. *'Single male.'*

I closed the holdall, switched off the light and quickly made my way back to the hallway.

'Looks like a pro. He used a card to get in – dark clothes, no hat. Couldn't see any night vision specs.'

He might just be a burglar trying his luck, but then again he might not be. I let myself out onto the landing, quietly pulling Rambart's door shut behind me. Whoever this person is they hadn't switched on any lights. I flicked down my night visions and crouched on the landing beside the top of the stairs. Anybody climbing the stairs couldn't see me there; maybe he'd go on past and up to the second or third floor. He didn't.

As he came off the stairs and round onto the landing, I stood and hit him as hard as I could in the face. He let out a stifled moan as he crumpled and hit the floor holding his broken nose, I stamped on his stomach. I never take chances, he was going to stay where he was, alternating between trying to get his breath back and stemming the blood and pain from a broken nose long after I'd gone.

I left the building and shut the street door behind me, Gold was crossing the road and walked close beside me as I dropped the night visions in to her shoulder bag. We separated and she dropped back into the crowd. I walked a further hundred metres along Knightsbridge, crossed the road and walked the same distance on the other side before crossing back and doing another hundred metres.

'You're clear,' came through my earpiece. I stopped and waited as Gold caught me up. The road crossings would have shown if anybody was tailing me.

'Do you know who he is?' she asked as I gave her my earpiece and battery pack which she put into the shoulder bag.

'No idea, just a chancer I suppose.'

'No, he wasn't a chancer.'

I looked at her. 'No?'

'No, I clocked him earlier today. He was dressed normally then, suit and briefcase, It didn't register with me at first 'cause he was looking in the shop window like any other person would but when a resident left the building he was quick to get to the door before it shut and go in – I thought maybe he was just another resident. He didn't stay inside long so I got a good look at his face when he left. That was him again tonight, all togged up for a job – I reckon he went in earlier to take a look at the layout and what the locks were. I take it he made for Rambart's apartment?'

'Well, he came onto her floor, yes – her landing. No other apartments on it, just hers.'

'So he was there for a reason.'

'Guns.'

'Guns?'

'That holdall you saw earlier is full of PPKs, maybe he was picking them up. I should have checked his pockets, he may have had a key.'

'So it looks like she's either arms dealing for herself or part of hubby's firm?'

'Both make sense.'

'Could be the million quid job offer is her takeover move to get rid of Nicholas. Are you sure you want to be part of that? Sounds a bit dangerous to me?'

'You could be right. I think I'll sleep on it and see if she hassles me – the forty-eight hours is up tomorrow.'

****

CHAPTER 3

'Well well well, this is a surprise.'

I looked up from the morning newspapers I'd been looking through for any mention of the previous night's escapade – nothing yet. The man stood before me in my office was Clarence Woodward – Commander Clarence Woodward, although he'd never been in any line of fire except from maybe a few expletives from the Home Secretary when things in MI6 go wrong. Woodward is a civil servant, he had progressed through the Ministry of Defence and then into MI6, quickly climbing the ladder to the top where he had been my boss during the latter part of my N14 service – N14 being the select group of individuals who did the jobs that even the SAS declined: political hits to assist regime change, destruction of enemy threats and nuclear progress installations, things like that. You would never know Woodward was anywhere near that stuff; slightly built, dark hair neatly combed back, fawn overcoat, pinstriped suit, regimental tie, shining brogues and always with his umbrella for company, he gave the immediate impression of 'somebody in the city'. Behind him his two bodyguards waited by the door. The common perception of a bodyguard is somebody the size of a barn door with hams for hands and no neck. Maybe that's true for the underworld but in the real world of espionage they are well trained, fit and intelligent. Just like me eh? Okay, maybe the 'fit' bit could do with a little tuning up.

Woodward pulled out a chair and blew away any dust before sitting and facing me. He didn't look amused; I got the impression from his expression this wasn't a social visit.

'Enjoyed yourself last night did you, Nevis?'

He sat back waiting for my answer. He wasn't going to get one, not before I understood how the hell he knew about my Rambart visit. After few seconds of silence he nodded towards the newspapers on my desk. 'You won't find any mention of your evening's work in there.' We held each other's gaze for another few seconds. 'You'll be glad to know he'll live – no major organ damage, a broken nose, three broken ribs and a perforated lung being the collateral damage caused by one of the ribs.' The silence fell for a while again before he continued. 'It was a classic unarmed combat attack, straight out of the textbook: hard hit to nose incapacitates the victim and if hard enough sends him to the floor. This *was* hard enough and *did* send him to the floor, where phase two – a good stamp on the stomach – winds the victim and leaves him basically paralysed whilst the attacked makes a getaway.'

I stayed silent. So Gold was right: the intruder was a pro, not a chancer but an MI6 operative. So were they onto Rambart or her husband, and the man I decked on his way to look for something in the apartment?

Woodward took out his iPhone and clicked on a video before passing it across the desk for me to view. I guessed what I was about to see. I was right. It was a video of me coming out of the Rambart building and crossing paths with Gold before walking out of shot along Knightsbridge.

Woodward pulled it back, turned it off and put it back in his pocket. 'Unfortunately it's only a static camera – no operator, we just download every twenty-four hours. We have lots of them around the capital – very small, ideal for surveillance of second degree suspects when manpower is stretched. The Rambarts are, or should I say *were*, second degree suspects – just a couple we liked to keep tabs on knowing the kind of business they are involved in. Every month or so we send a man in to do a physical check on the premises, just in case a bomb factory has started up – can't be too careful. The next visit wasn't due until next week, but on checking the footage our people saw a holdall and two characters on our surveillance list go in during the afternoon so we brought the visit forward. Of course, after the unsavoury incident on the stairs we reviewed the video, and hey presto! You and the Gold Digger make an appearance, or should I say exit. So putting that together with the type of attack our chap endured, I would say the circumstantial evidence points to you. Assault and battery – nasty episode, five years minimum.'

I reached for the phone. He guessed my reaction.

'Don't bother, you don't need a lawyer. I don't think I mentioned anything about pressing charges, did I?' Woodward smiled, the sort of smile your chess opponent gives when he's made a move that says '*checkmate*'. 'I have no intention of pressing charges. I want to know why you were there Nevis, that's all.'

Time to break my silence, 'Eve Rambart came and asked me to do some security work for her – she'd been recommended. I was just checking the premises out, seeing what alarm system would be best, checking the locks. She said somebody had tried to break in recently so when your man showed up I thought it was the same person coming back,' I lied, hoping it sounded reasonable. I didn't think I'd better mention the small matter of a million quid to kill hubby.

Woodward shifted in his chair and let out a long breath. 'I'm going to take you into my confidence Nevis, and if any of this makes its way into the public domain I will have no problem in pressing the charges I spoke about and making sure your PI Licence is revoked, understand me?'

I nodded.

'Good. We have had the Rambarts under surveillance for some time – we know her husband supplies Iran with illegal arms, and they then send those arms onto ISIS, Al-Qaeda and other terrorist groups in the Middle East. We need to know how they get there. Of course diplomatic channels have put pressure on Iran, but their denials are just the normal lies; the Revolutionary Guard have no scruples, and their main *raison d'etre* is to basically blow up the West so if they can supply arms to terrorist groups they will. However, recently their armaments have got more sophisticated and include missiles capable of being nuclear tipped for both ground and air launching. We have evidence that Rambart is the supplier. He doesn't handle the product himself, he's too clever to take that chance – he is a middle man between supplier and buyer. He is also the *legal* middle man between suppliers and buyers in the West, which is how we think he operates. He fuses the two, buys on behalf of a Western country or a Western Allied Middle Eastern country, which enables him to get his orders signed off by the governments of the Arms Suppliers countries without any fuss – the UK Ministry of Defence included – and then the product gets diverted on route to countries that are not signed up to the Non-Proliferation Treaty.'

'And the original country doesn't ask *where are our missiles*?'

'Depends – depends how much their current Minister of Defence takes in bribe money and showers around to keep eyes closed and mouths shut. Sometimes if it is a genuine order that goes AWOL and into Rambart's plan the country won't want it known as the news of such a loss they would mean they certainly wouldn't get authority to purchase anymore.'

'Why are you telling me all this?'

'You're going to work for us.'

'I am?'

'Either that or time in one of Her Majesty's establishments awaits you and the SIA will revoke your PI licence. Your choice Nevis.'

'Looks like I'm working for you then.'

Woodward gave another *checkmate* smile, 'Good, I thought you might prefer that. It's a very simple job: get inside the Rambarts' organisation and feed back their contacts and their buyers to me – and most importantly find Nicholas Rambart; he's gone off the radar for the past three months, disappeared, which means he's putting together a big deal somewhere and doesn't want to be disturbed. That's worrying us, it means he's probably handling armaments he's not licensed to handle. He is the top suspect for supplying the missiles that destroyed Saudi Arabia's oil tanks and if one of his terrorist friends are planning a similar attack who knows where it could be. We and the US have operatives looking for him, but so far we haven't located him. You now have an inside position in the family as Eve Rambart's security advisor and that could be our best shot yet. You are of course nothing to do with the department, and if anything untoward happens to you we will deny even knowing who you are.'

I was beginning to regret saying I was working for Eve Rambart, but circumstances and video footage had pushed me into a position I didn't want to be in. I had no exit.

'That was always normal procedure, nothing new in that.'

'Quite, and you report directly to me.'

'To you?' That was surprising as MI6 operatives usually have a handler as a point of contact, not the big boss.

'Yes, to me and me only. There will not be any leaks on this assignment Nevis.' He reached into his suit pocket and pulled out a burner phone which he put on the desk. 'This phone is programmed to go straight through to me, just press the call button – it has a lithium battery so you'll get five days continual use before it needs charging. The number it calls is my personal phone, which is programmed to take your call and override any other call that I may be taking at the time. If it looks like it might fall into other people's hands at anytime, press 999 and all call logs on it will be cancelled and scrambled.'

'And no doubt it has a tracing app installed?' I knew it would have – of course it would have. Woodward wanted to know where I was, of course he did.

He just smiled and rose to leave.

'Whoa.' I had one item for discussion. He turned back to me and I held out a hand, rubbing my thumb and forefinger together. 'You forgot to mention?'

He smiled. 'Remuneration? You haven't changed Nevis, have you? I seem to remember you were always the one with, shall we say, rather high expense claims?'

'Can't live on fresh air and doing one's duty to the country alone.'

'Five thousand a week...' He had second thoughts, 'No, six thousand a week and no expense claims.'

'Okay,' It wasn't a great deal compared with what I could earn from the likes of Jameson Reynolds, but I was already thinking ahead to the endgame of a million pound hit on Mr Nicholas Rambart; for MI6 to be paying for my time whilst I was reconnoitring and assessing how to achieve that suited me just fine. 'My bank details are still the same. I'll be checking every week.' I gave him my copy of his *checkmate* smile.

'I hope to hear from you within forty eight hours, Nevis,' he said, and gave one last nod and a smile and left flanked by his two bodyguards

Forty-eight hours, where had I heard that before? Time to tell Mrs Rambart she had a deal, but first I'd better call Gold and tell her to clear her diary, we've got work to do.

****

CHAPTER 4

'Shit.'

Gold looked over to the table where her phone had started buzzing. One look told her it was Nevis. She put down the horsewhip she was holding and answered it.

'Yeah?'

'I've got news, we are now in the pay of MI6 at five grand a week.'

'We are?'

'You'd best come over, I don't want to talk on the phone.'

'I'm working.'

'Oh, okay – come over when you're finished. Anybody I know?'

'Lord Herbert of Chantbury.'

Nevis laughed. 'Is he still alive?'

'Just about. I'll come over now, His Lordship can wait.' She shut the phone, picked up her shoulder bag from the table and put the whip on it, collected her coat from the chair she'd draped it over, counted out two hundred pounds in tenners from the five hundred on the table, moved over to the bedroom door and shouted through it, 'Sorry Lord Herbert, gotta go – family business. I'll call next week,' and quickly made her way out of Lord Herbert of Chantbury's Belgravia apartment.

His Lordship emerged from the bedroom in an ill-fitting maid's uniform, high heels and an overdone application of rouge on his cheeks and stared bewilderedly at the door.

****

CHAPTER 5

'I didn't think you would be able to resist,' Eve Rambart spoke into her mobile. She was standing at the front window of the apartment looking down onto Knightsbridge below. 'You can't come here, too many of my husband's people are around here. I'm sure he has them watching me. Apparently there was an unsavoury incident inside the apartment block last night – probably a rough sleeper getting beaten up. I don't know the ins and outs of it, but if any of my husband's people had found him near the apartment he'd be lucky to still be alive. You understand what I am saying, Mr Nevis – my husband moves in particularly nasty circles, his business involves such people. I know you are well-versed in that sort of company – no disrespect meant by that remark – but that and your past military career as told to me by Jameson Reynolds is why I paid *you* a visit. You will be getting into dangerous waters, Mr Nevis – waters with hungry sharks in residence. I have to go to my bank in the morning, Coutts in the Strand – I will be there at ten. If you are there we can transfer a retainer into your bank account – I think two hundred thousand should be about right? Returnable of course, if your mission fails. And don't forget,

Mr Nevis, I move in the same circles as my husband and know people who would answer to me should you try any silly business with the money. No completion of the job means no money, understand?'

She didn't wait for an answer and closed her phone.

****

Nevis closed his phone and looked across the office desk at Gold who raised her eyebrows.

'Well?'

'Two hundred grand, up front.'

'Nice.'

'And it stays in my account until we complete the hit. If anything goes tits-up I don't want her people coming round for a refund of money that's not there.'

'Okay, so all we have to do is find her old man now and bang bang.' She made the shape of a gun with her hand.

****

The business at the bank went okay – mind you, I got some funny looks from the manager who handled the transaction. Might have been my

Status Quo T-shirt and faded jeans, they didn't seem to fit the opulent Coutts Bank offices; the antique mahogany furniture, hushed tones and dark-suited staff. He raised his eyebrows when I gave the account I wanted the money sent to.

'Lloyds Bank in Southwark?'

'Correct.'

'Are you sure, sir?'

'I'm sure.'

He obviously was more used to such amounts being transferred to offshore tax havens or maybe Middle Eastern banks. He printed off a receipt for the transaction and another for Eve Rambart and she thanked him and we walked out of the dim bank interior into the bright sunshine in the Strand. A shiny black Merc with tinted passenger windows pulled over and stopped as we walked out. The driver in chauffeur's uniform got out and came round to open the rear door.

'I don't want to hear from you again until you have completed the job, Mr Nevis. Do not contact me under any circumstances, understood? If I think I have anything that will help you I will text you.'

'Okay,' I nodded. 'But don't hassle me – these kind of jobs have to be planned and can take a while.'

She laughed. 'I won't hassle you, Mr Nevis. But the sooner it is done, the sooner another eight hundred thousand pounds makes its way to Southwark.' And with a beaming smile she got into the car and was gone.

'Nice car,' Gold said as she joined me from across the road where she'd been covering me.

'Get the number?'

'Yes, I'll get an ex of mine to run it through ANPR.'

****

CHAPTER 6

Well, where do you start looking for a man even MI6 can't find? I sat down in my office the next morning and started on a computer search: his background, his companies, their files at Companies House, any relatives – anything at all. He was obviously a private man; one who valued his privacy greatly as the only lead I could find was a paparazzi picture of him and Eve at Ascot three years ago, and that wasn't much help as the top hat and large sunglasses kept most of his head and face hidden. I hoped Gold was having more luck; she was twisting arms and pulling strings with her contacts in the upper class echelon of her '*client*' list. It had worked for us before; household names and celebrities were always most keen to help when shown snippets of videos Gold had of them in scenarios they really wouldn't want released on social media. Button cameras can be so useful.

I pulled up the Ascot picture on my Adobe, cropped it to just Nicholas Rambart's face, enlarged it and printed it off. I sat back and studied it. *Where oh where are you now, Mr Rambart?*

The answer came quickly as the man himself, preceded and followed by two rather large gentlemen in long overcoats and dark glasses came into the office. No words were spoken whilst one of his goons checked the kitchen was empty; the other one stood outside the office door assuring his master of undisturbed privacy. I recognised the one checking the kitchen even behind his dark glasses: Grant Rankin, ex-Sergeant Grant Rankin, Met's Organised Crime Squad. I never worked with Rankin but he had the reputation as a bit of a loner; kept himself to himself and spent most of the time I knew him deep underground, mixing amongst the East London Eastern European population where organised crime gangs from Romania were embedded. He had Iranian parents who fled when the IRGC started persecuting academics – both were teachers; he'd obviously quit the Met and gone into private security like me.

'It says knock,' I said, pointing at the notice on my door, and then sat back and crossed my arms, hoping to give out a relaxed image.

Nicholas Rambart took the chair opposite me and pointed to the printout. He smiled, 'Ascot 1919.'

'Did you back a winner?' Well, what else could I say? There I was caught bang to rights looking at his mug shot.

He smiled. 'I did not – I don't gamble, Mr Nevis. However, it seems you do.'

I raised my eyebrows and gave a slight tilt to my head. 'I do?'

'Yes, and I fear you have backed a loser in Eve, my wife,' his turn to raise the eyebrows and look at me for an answer. I stayed silent. How much did he know of the deal with Eve Rambart? Did he know anything at all other than she had been here, or was he fully aware of our arrangement? And more importantly, would I get out of here alive if he did? The goon at the office door didn't look the sort that took prisoners.

Rambart sat back and let out a long breath. 'She wants me dead, doesn't she Mr Nevis? She would have told you that and offered a considerable sum of money for you to carry out the...' He paused, searching for the word; he found it. 'The *hit* – I think that is the term you people use, *hit*.' He shook his head a little, side to side like a headmaster would when wondering what to do with a repeatedly naughty child. 'Trouble is, Mr Nevis, you took the money, so I assume you *do* intend to kill me.' He held up a hand to silence me as I was about to concoct some sort of denial. 'Please don't deny it, not unless you have a copper-bottomed reason for your visit to Coutts yesterday and the money transfer?'

I should have known; a man in his position would have all the angles covered. The bank manger probably made a call as soon as we had left; maybe the chauffeur was a plant put there to keep an eye on the wife? It didn't matter, Nicholas Rambart knew I had taken a payment to kill him. I had my Walther PK380 in the desk drawer, but would I get to it before one of his men got me? I should probably have a go, as it was obvious I wasn't going to be allowed to make good on my deal with Eve Rambart. I uncrossed my arms, ready to go for the drawer.

Rambart stroked his chin, sensing the change in my body language. 'No, Mr Nevis, I am not going to kill you. In fact, I quite admire you for taking the job; she asked four other people before you and they all refused. You must be very confident in your ability to complete the job – either that or you must be very hard up. I think it's the first, I think you have confidence in your ability. I like that in people, Mr Nevis, I could use more people like that in my organisation. In fact, I am going to offer you a job.'

'You are?'

'Yes, a very simple job that will wipe the slate clean between us; and, if you accept it and complete it, you will never hear from me, or wife, again. That's a promise, and I always keep my promises.' He took a deep breath before continuing with a sad shake of his head. 'Unfortunately, love is blind, Mr Nevis. You have met my wife – who wouldn't fall in love with such a creature? But only in the harsh light of day after the honeymoon, one comes to realise that the inside of a person is not all they seem on the outside. With her two previous husbands in the ground I do not intend to become my wife's next financial benefactor and little mourned third husband. I want you to kill my wife, and I will give you one million pounds when you do.'

I was stunned. I had two people both wanting me to kill each other, and both willing to pay big money for it. I hadn't any choice with Nicholas Rambart's offer, it wasn't negotiable – I took the job or I was brown bread. No way would he let me out of this office if I refused; I'd probably go out as a stiff rolled up in my own rather threadbare carpet, be weighted down and dropped into the Thames under cover of darkness, or maybe taken somewhere else more convenient to be incinerated or dumped into a vat of acid. I only had the one option if I wanted to live.

'I have no choice, do I?' I said in a resigned manner.

'No, you don't. Giving people choices is not my stock in trade, Mr Nevis, and obviously you wish to continue living – so no, you are right, you have no choice.' He stood and looked down at me. 'There is no time limit on it, Mr Nevis, but I would hope you would have completed the task in a month. If not, I may get a little worried – and I can assure you, Mr Nevis, you don't want that.' And with a curt nod of the head, he and his goons were gone.

It took me several minutes of thought, weighing up my options to come to the conclusion that I didn't have any – well, just one really, I had to kill Eve Rambart or I was as good as dead myself, and I had to kill Nicholas Rambart or lose a million quid, and maybe have her come after me. On top of that had to keep my word to Woodward, or I was bound for the Scrubs. Amazing how your life can change completely in a few days. I called Gold.

'Yeah?'

'What's happening?'

'I'm following your guests.'

I didn't understand. 'What do you mean?'

'I'd pulled up down the road on my way in to your office and saw the three of them get out of a posh limo and go in the building. Pretty obvious they weren't the sort of visitor you normally have, so I took a peep and saw the one standing guard outside your door, did an about turn and waited in my car. I guess you had a visit from Mr Rambart?'

'Yes.'

'Okay, don't tell me about it now as I'm following their limo – we are going through Streatham. I'll give you a call when we arrive at wherever it is we're going.'

'Okay, take care. My first impression is that he's not a very nice man.'

****

CHAPTER 7

Night was lowering its dark blanket as I pulled up behind Gold's car on an unlit road on a large industrial estate in Purley. She had texted me the street name and my sat nav had done its job. I slipped out of my car and into hers.

'I'm starving,' was the greeting I got. 'What did you bring?'

I gave her the egg mayonnaise sandwich and an orange drink carton I'd bought on the way; she'd asked me to bring food and drink as she hadn't had either since the morning and now it was late. I could have got there earlier but I wanted to take a good look at this place, and I worked best in the dark.

'See that big grey warehouse building at the end of the street?' she mumbled through a mouth full of egg mayonnaise. 'That's where they went. There's a security pod at the gate so if we want to take a good look around it'll have to be from the side or back. This estate is pretty new so I would assume the buildings have good alarm systems.'

I agreed, 'If Rambart is dealing arms I would bet he's got a state of the art one installed. You stay here I'm going for a walk round.'

'Not without these you're not,' she said, hauling her shoulder bag over from the back seat and giving me the earpiece, mic and battery belt pack. I set myself up as she did the same and we tested it. All systems go, we could hear each other and talk to each other.

I left the car and walked towards the building, I often thought I should get a dog – people wouldn't take any notice of a bloke walking his dog, but a bloke walking on his own in an industrial estate at night could create some interest from security people.

The gatehouse, or security pod as Gold had called it, was very professional, sitting behind a pair of solid metal bar twelve foot-high gates that opened on runners set in the concrete ground. Floodlights from the roof of the warehouse twenty meters behind illuminated the whole area, and their glare blinded my view of it. What must be Rambart's car was parked at the side of the gatehouse. I waited outside the scope of the floodlights, trying to make out who was in the gatehouse; I could only see one uniformed guard, and he was reading a book.

I crossed to the farthest point from the light and quickly moved through it back into the darkness of the street past the gates. I followed the high security chain-link fence around the compound; judging by the razor wire threaded along the top of it they really didn't want any visitors. I must have walked a hundred metres before the compound ended and butted against the next warehouse unit; a large *For Sale or Rent* sign on the front gave me hope that this might be a way in. No towering chain-link fence and razor wire fronted this unit, just a six foot breeze block wall. I was over that in seconds and stood in the gloom, getting my bearings. The block wall separated the unit from Rambart's unit, and a twisting curl of razor wire had been strung along the top of it; I needed a cover to throw over it. A tarpaulin spread over a heap of builder's sand dumped by the wall was ideal; I cut it into a four foot wide strip and folded it three times – razor wire is what it says on the tin: razor sharp.

Standing on the rest of the tarpaulin on top of the sand pile I threw the strip over the razor wire and eased myself up, crawling over and dropping down into Rambart's compound. I crouched and waited for alarms connected to movement sensors to wail, or the snarling barks or loose guard dogs coming at me, their open jaws salivating with expectation. Neither. I gave Gold a call.

'I'm in.'

'Good, all quiet at the front.'

I moved silently across the concrete to the building, a modern all metal prefabricated type; no windows as far as I could see, probably two storeys high stretching above me. Keeping close and moving to the nearest corner, I peeped round – same again: concrete road, no floodlights, no windows. Eureka! halfway along, a door. The handle was the type that had a Yale lock embedded in it. Tough to crack, say the adverts – so tough it took me all of twenty seconds before the audible click of the hammers aligning told me my picks had worked. Trouble was that this door was bound to be alarmed; open it and lights would flash on the gatehouse monitor board. At least that's what I hoped – I certainly didn't want any loud alarm going off screaming into the night. Fifty-fifty chance, but having got this far I was going to take the chance.

'Gold.'

'Yes?'

'I'm going in a door, but it's bound to be alarmed – I'm banking on it triggering something in the gatehouse. Can you create a diversion? I could only see one bloke in there, I need to get him out for a couple of minutes.'

'Will do, I'll give you a call when it's clear.'

I knelt down by the door and waited. I reckoned that if all Hell broke loose I could be back to the wall and over it in about twenty seconds. I waited for Gold.

****

Getting out of her car Gold removed her coat and pulled on a beret covering her hair. She walked towards the gates, giving a few staggers on the way; Gold was making like a young lady who had slightly too much drink inside her. She wobbled to the gates and shook them. The guard looked up from his book and waved her to go away. She shook the gates more and blew him kisses. He didn't move, just waved his hand for her to go and shook his head in despair at the young of today – drink and drugs, this girl's parents should be ashamed.

Gold was a bit worried. When she'd tried this trick before, a young lady slightly drunk had always brought more attention than this guard was giving. Plan B then, that always worked.

She reached under her jumper and released her bra, then pulling it out waved it at the guard. Now she had his attention, oh yes – and when she raised her jumper and flashed a firm pair of breasts, his eyes nearly left their sockets.

But the bastard wouldn't leave his chair, let alone the gatehouse!

Gold moved up against the gates and pressed her chest against one so that her breasts poked through either side of a metal bar. Christ it was cold, but things were heating up in the gatehouse; the guard had stood up and was on his way out of the door.

'All clear, go.'

She knew she had to keep that guard out of that gatehouse until Nevis had killed the alarm switch. It was now a game of cat and mouse with the guard to keep him at the gate until Nevis said: 'Clear.'

****

I got the *all clear, go* from Gold.

I turned the door handle and pushed the door slowly open and slipped inside. No screaming alarms, so it was a silent one to the gatehouse security board; it could also go straight through to the police, but I didn't think Nicholas Rambart would want them on the premises so probably not. The warehouse inside was dimly lit, but I didn't give it much attention as I had to get this door alarm knocked out. Just as I thought, it had a standard keypad on the wall next to it – the lights would be flashing in the gatehouse by now. I took out my mobile and pressed on the Apps list, and then the one I'd named FP – *finger print.* I took a close-up picture of the keypad and hit go; almost instantaneously four numbers flashed onto the screen. These were the four numbers with the most patination on the keyboard – patination being the microparticles of dust and dirt clinging to the fingerprint oil on the four numbers that had been hit the most times. I had the numbers, but in which order? I hoped the numbers 1 and 9 were there – they were. It's a known fact that people use birthdays when setting alarm codes, and the person who set this one would have been born in the twentieth century, so would use 19. The other two numbers were 7 and 8. I keyed them in, got it right first time: 1978 – well, thank you and happy birthday whoever you are. The bleeping red light on the keypad turned green, and I hoped the same had happened on the gatehouse board.

I called Gold. 'All clear, I'm in.'

****

Thank Heaven for that, thought Gold as the message hit her earpiece. She'd been playing *try and touch my tits* with the guard, who had an arm through the gate slats as she proffered a breast and pulled it away after the slightest of touches, giggling like a drunk girl. Luckily the guard was late middle-aged and wasn't very nifty.

'You're a naughty man,' Gold slurred at him. 'I'm going home and maybe I'll come back tomorrow. What time do you get off?'

'Eight in the morning, come back then.' The guard's speech was shaking with hope.

Gold gave him a wave and wandered off out of his view and back to her car. 'Jesus, Ben,' she said to herself as she reinstated her bra. – 'The things I do for you. I hope there's no CCTV of the gate, or my tits will be all over social media in no time,'

****

CHAPTER 8

I knelt by the side of the door as my eyes got accustomed to the dim light. The place seemed much bigger inside than it had looked from the outside. The floor was covered in wooden crates of all sizes, the smaller ones stacked halfway up to the roof, the large ones resting on pallets for easy movement by forklift truck. Four forklifts were parked up along the wall from me, their batteries being charged through wall plugs. There didn't seem to be anybody about – no noise, no movement between the crates. Time to take a closer look for Woodward. I took out the mobile he'd given me, turned off the automatic flash and moving slowly between the crates, I took pictures of the labels stuck on them. I reckoned there was enough light for them to be read; they weren't in English, some looked to be in an Eastern European language and some Middle Eastern.

The sound of voices sent me hitting the floor between two large crates. What the hell, how had I missed people being here? I hadn't missed them – they weren't here on the floor, they were upstairs. In a far corner at the back of the warehouse a steel staircase led up to an office perched on a mezzanine platform. The office door was open and light flooded out; the windows to the office were covered inside with blinds, so no light would have shown before. I breathed a sigh of relief; I could have been caught lock stock and barrel. I kicked myself for being so lax. I could have been seen from up there, but the office had been hidden from my sightline from the door by stacked crates. I stayed prone on the floor, listening; I counted four voices, not speaking in English and the metallic clanking said they were coming down the staircase. I pulled out my gun. If I was discovered here, a hands up and *'sorry'* wouldn't keep me alive, no way. I screwed the silencer onto the barrel.

The footsteps down the staircase had stopped, and the voices were moving farther away from me through the crates towards the front of the warehouse. That was a relief. A door slammed shut. I was on my own – or was I? I'd thought that before. What if there was somebody else left up in the office? I peeped up from behind the crate. The office was in darkness, but the door was shut so who knows what was inside? I'd better alert Gold.

'People have left the warehouse – could be Rambart. Four of them.'

'I've got them, four including Rambart – he and one other getting into his limo. Looks

like they are leaving, the other two staying. I'll follow.'

'Okay, I'm going to have a look around. I'll call you on the mobile when I'm out.' The comms would only pick up for half a mile, so Gold would soon be out of range.

I looked at the steel staircase leading from the floor up to the office; I would be in full view of the whole warehouse going up it and an easy target. Fingers crossed there weren't any other people around that might come in and see me. I moved through the crates to the bottom of it and started up, quickly but silently. At the top I crouched by the door and listened – the rule was you listen for three minutes, as on average a person will move within three minutes. After two I was satisfied I was alone. The door didn't have a keyhole – that spelled danger; could be it takes a key fob to open it like a car, could be it has a magnetic close and once that breaks an alarm operates? Only one way to find out.

I pushed it open quickly and stepped inside, crouching with my gun held steady with both hands in front of me. The office was empty, no alarm was sounding, and no CCTV was watching from the ceiling or walls. I decided not to turn the light on and flicked on my head torch and began a search of the desk drawers. Lots of legal looking papers in a foreign language. I clicked away with Woodward's camera. There was a safe in the corner, but I didn't have time to work on that – locks I can do, safes are bit beyond me, but I took a picture of it in case Woodward wanted me to come back with somebody who could open it.

I spent at least ten minutes in that room taking snaps of papers in folders in a filing cabinet – far too many to snap them all but I took five of the first pages in each of the folders. The filing cabinet had been locked, but come on – a lock on a filing cabinet is easy for a kid, let alone a pro. I had laughed as it popped open after about five seconds' work with the picks – oh Mr Rambart, maybe you should employ me as a security consultant.

Loud footsteps and voices on the metal staircase sent a shiver through me, I clicked on the comms, hoping Gold was still within reach.

'Confirm how many are in the car?' I asked quietly.

'Two, why?'

'There were four in the warehouse and I think I have the other two back for company.'

'Want me back?'

'No, surprise is on my side.' I put my gun in my pocket – I didn't think I'd need it – and turned off my head torch. I checked that all my pockets were shut – good old Velcro, I didn't want anything that could identify me falling out.

The door was an inward opening one, so the best attack would be to hit them whilst they were on the stairs; I would have the height advantage and they would naturally be off balance. I pulled my balaclava down to full facial and pulled the door open quietly. They were at the top step and being a narrow staircase were one behind the other. I stepped out as the first one stepped up onto the platform and raised my leg and planted my right boot into his stomach with force. The look of surprise on his face was immediately followed by one of fear mixed with pain as he fell back onto number two, and they both tumbled back down the staircase, their bodies and heads banging against the steel handrails and steps as they fell.

I was down after them in a flash and had the first one lifted up and over the rail in a split second. I didn't bother to watch him fall as number two was getting himself together and although laid sideways on the stairs was reaching into a coat pocket, probably for a gun. I jumped the three steps down to him and stamped on his other hand that was clinging to the step; he squealed in pain as the finger tendons snapped under my boot. I took him by the hair and smashed his head into the handrail a couple of times before lifting his now limp body up and over to plummet to the floor below to join number one.

I took the stairs in twos to the bottom and hurried to where my victims had fallen, pulling out my gun just in case. Number one was draped over the edge of a large crate and there was a fair amount of blood seeping into the wood; his pulse was dead, and so was he. Number two had hit the concrete floor and was amazingly stirring and moving – couldn't have that, no witnesses is how I work. I put his neck in an arm lock and twisted until the jolt and crack told me he was gone too. I know what you are thinking, and you are right – I'm not a very nice man when the chips are down, but that's probably why I'm still alive and in one piece. Six years undercover behind the Taliban lines in Afghanistan teaches you that he who attacks first usually wins.

A fair amount of noise had been made during all this, so I moved quickly away to a far corner and sat out of sight behind a crate, getting my breath back and waiting to see if there was anybody else around who might have heard something and be coming to investigate. I gave it a couple of minutes – all quiet, time to go.

Getting out was a damn sight easier than getting in now that I had the code to the side door. I shut it behind me, clicking the lock into position; nobody would know I'd come in that way and once over the wall I lifted the tarpaulin off the razor wire and put it back over the sand heap. The razor wire looked a bit flat and anybody checking would see that there was where the intruder got in, but that didn't make any odds really – I was out.

I kept in the dark and made my way back to my car; the guard in the gatehouse was sitting at his table reading. I wondered how Gold had coaxed him out? No doubt she'd tell me later. She didn't.

I drove out of the industrial estate and tried the comms; no reply, she was obviously out of its reach so I gave her a call on the mobile.

'What's happening? Where are you?'

'Coming up to Marble Arch, they haven't stopped on the way.'

'Okay, stay with them – he must be going home for the night so we could get a break on where he lives.'

'He might be going to the Knightsbidge place. How did you get on, are you out?'

'Yes, got a lot of photos of crates and papers for Woodward. He should be happy.'

‘You leave a mess behind?’

‘Nah, you know me – a couple of bodies, that’s all.’

‘Typical. I hope one of them wasn’t the guard from the front gate, that would have spoilt his best shift ever.’

‘Really, how come?’

‘I’ll tell you some other time, or maybe I won’t. Hey ho! It’s not Knightsbridge, we’re off up Park Lane.’

‘Okay, call me when you stop at wherever it is they’re going.’

‘Will do.’

I thought it best to avoid my office; once the bodies were found I could expect a visit from Rambart. Nothing I had said to him could tie me into it, but he might think it highly coincidental his warehouse got a visit so soon after his visit to me – well, wouldn’t you?

Gold didn’t call me until I was home and brewing up a coffee – home being a two bedroom apartment in a modern serviced block overlooking the Thames and Jubilee gardens at Waterloo. Costs a bomb, but being serviced nobody gets in that doesn’t live here, and anybody visiting has to get past the security chaps on the door who ring up for permission first. That way I know who’s coming up and know who – if anybody – has been asking for me. Nobody had tonight. The underground car park also gave a separate way out if I ever needed to leave without using the main doors. Well you never know, do you? The final piece of my security was that the apartment was not leased in my name – George Hadlow was who I was registered as with the landlord. George was the first name I'd come across on a gravestone in a great plague cemetery off the York Road. Nobody would be able to trace him, that's for sure. A man I know who knows another man who knows a man who does fake passports and credit cards provided me with all the documentation and references I needed to secure the lease. It's not what you know in this world, it's who you know.

****

CHAPTER 9

Gold was following Rambart's car off Park Lane and through a side street before it turned off and disappeared down a ramp into the Hilton Hotel car park. She couldn't follow as the barrier was key card protected, so she drove on and found a place to park a few hundred yards away; double yellow lines, but Nevis could pay if there was a ticket on her windscreen when she came back. She hurried to the hotel; it was busy – very busy. A coach load of tourists were signing in; not much chance of spotting Rambart and the other man in this crowd, but she did the rounds and checked the restaurants and bars in the hope she'd see them. No joy. Oh well, plan B then.

She walked through the foyer to the ground floor corridors that led to the rooms. As she expected, the half moon side tables at corridor junctions each had a vase with a large bunch of fresh flowers in the middle. She stopped at one, checked around to make sure she was alone and lifted the flowers out, wrapped their stalks in the small table covering cloth and made her way to Reception. The Reception desk was very busy – good, that meant they wouldn't want to waste time on a delivery girl. She approached the nearest receptionist and interrupted her dealings with a resident signing in.

'Delivery for Mrs Rambart,' she said with a smile. 'The lady must have an admirer.'

The receptionist returned the smile – she didn't really want to, she'd rather tell this courier to piss off or wait at the back of the queue. But she wasn't allowed to express her real feelings, not in this job – best to get rid of the pest. 'We haven't any staff free at the moment you'll have to take them up yourself if she's in. Sorry.'

Gold nodded. 'Okay, I'll have to be quick though – taxi's waiting.'

The receptionist checked her screen. 'What is the name?'

'Rambart.'

'You're in luck, it's occupied. 324, it's a suite on the third floor,'

Gold nodded her thanks and made her way to the lifts. There was a crowd waiting for them so she took the stairs and on the first floor dumped the flowers on the first table in the corridor and made her way out of the hotel and back to her car. No ticket.

****

I was taking my first sip of a welcome cup of coffee and just switched on the TV when Gold called.

'He's got a suite at the Hilton.'

'Really? Living the life, eh?'

'Yes, they drove into the Hilton car park so I had to park about a bloody mile away and walk back. I checked the Reception area and restaurants – couldn't see them, but it was busy so I could have missed them. I nicked a bunch of flowers out of a vase and played the delivery scam – he's in suite 324.'

I was surprised. Top class hotel reception staff wouldn't fall for the delivery scam and would never give out room information; apparently the Hilton isn't a top class hotel.

'Good work,' I congratulated her. 'I'll check tomorrow and see if it's a permanent booking – probably is. You want to sleep here tonight?'

'No, I've got a few things to do at home. You in the office tomorrow?'

'No, I'm going to play safe and stay away for a couple of days. Once Rambart hears about the goings on at his warehouse he might want to have a chat with me.'

'Yes, probably would. Okay, I'll see you for lunch at the usual place about one tomorrow. I've got some unfinished business with Lord Herbert of Chantbury to sort out in the morning.'

I laughed. 'Okay, take care.'

I sat back and taking Woodward's mobile from my pocket I sent him the pictures from the warehouse. He wouldn't be able to say I was slacking on the job.

****

CHAPTER 10

The *usual place* for lunch with Gold was the cafe on the concourse at Charing Cross station; not the kind of place to take anybody you were trying to impress, but the food wasn't bad and a window table gave a good view of anybody coming towards it. You can't be too careful. Golden rule in my game, always meet in crowded public places, there's safety in numbers and you don't stand out, nobody notices you.

We sat there with our fish and chips and talked over the previous day's work. I had checked the local radio and television news stations and the South London press, but no mention of my warehouse escapade of the night before.

'Rambart obviously doesn't want the coppers inside the place,' Gold said, trying to shake some tomato sauce from an obstinate bottle. 'Two murders in a warehouse would have them crawling all over it by now if it was legit.'

'Self defence, not murders,' I corrected her.

'Oh yeah? No jury would ever believe that if they knew you.' Rather more tomato sauce than she needed decided to leave the bottle and overwhelm her piece of fish. 'Shit!'

My mobile buzzed. It was Woodward.

'We need to meet.'

I looked at Gold and covered the phone. 'Woodward wants to meet, you okay with that?'

'No – nobody knows I work with you and that's how I want it to stay. Give us twenty minutes to finish lunch and have a coffee and then meet him here. I'll be around.'

I nodded. If Gold thought Woodward doesn't know we work together she's wrong, but I didn't say anything and went back to Woodward on the phone. 'I'm not in my office – giving it a wide berth for a few days. I'm going to get something to eat in half an hour at the cafe on Charing Cross Station, how does that sound?'

'Sounds pretty ghastly, but I'll see you there in thirty minutes.'

The phone went dead.

'He's coming here, thirty minutes.'

'Okay.' Gold had cleared the sauce off her fish and was tucking in. 'Should be interesting.' She pointed her knife at me to make a point,' You've got a couple of decisions to make Ben, and Woodward being in the picture doesn't exactly make them any easier.'

'Decisions?'

'Well, for a start you have a contract on both the Rambarts – which one are you going to honour? The way I see it, if you hit Eve

Rambart you lose eighty grand, and if you hit Nicholas Rambart you lose a million. From the money side of things you should hit Eve and end up with a million from Nicholas, plus the two hundred thousand Eve's paid already.'

'If he pays up and doesn't have me killed.'

'There's always that scenario. You should have taken an advance of him too. These chips are cold.' She put her cutlery down onto the plate, wiped her mouth with a tissue from her shoulder bag and gave me a '*make your choice*' smile. 'Right, I'm going to dig a bit more into Eve Rambart. I've a feeling something's not quite right with her.' She stood and swung the bag onto her shoulder. 'I'll call you later.' And she was gone, merging into the commuters outside.

My chips were okay, so I finished my meal and fetched a coffee from the counter. Two sips in and Woodward stood in front of me, a disdainful look on his face; nobody could look more out of place in the Charing Cross Station cafe than Clarence Woodward. He took a handkerchief from his light brown overcoat and flapped it at the seat before sitting down. I fought hard to keep from smiling too broadly.

'I shall refrain from passing comment on your choice of meeting place, Nevis – suffice to say it wouldn't have been mine.'

'Can I get you a coffee?'

'Good Heavens no, I shouldn't think the coffee here has been within a thousand miles of a coffee bean.' He undid the top button of his coat and pulled out a printed paper from his inside pocket. 'You did have some fun last night didn't you, eh?' He didn't wait for a reply. 'We've had the Purley warehouse under surveillance for some time – your antics there were seen and watched, although apparently those of a young lady working with you were far more interesting to our chaps than yours, but we won't go into that. I take it she is the one known in certain circles as Gold Digger?'

'I have no idea what you are talking about.'

He smiled. 'Of course you don't. Anyway, it seems two bodies were removed from the premises shortly after the arrival of the day shift this morning – the day shift that comprises of a minibus of illegal immigrants who are kept in a house a few miles away in Croydon. You see Nevis, we do have an idea what is going on with Rambart inside that warehouse, although it all seems perfectly legal on the outside; but we don't have enough information to get a warrant issued and take a look. No need for a warrant now – your photos confirm our worst fears. Rambart is an arms dealer; a perfectly honest one on the outside, licensed annually, always gets the necessary export documents for the product he moves – all above board. But unfortunately he exceeds his license; he's very clever and we have not been able to nab him so far, but these photos show us a crack in his operation where we may be able to get in and bring him down.'

'They do?' I should have gone for more than five grand a month.

'Yes, indeed they do. The markings on the crates are Turkish – the crates are destined for Cyprus. As I am sure you are aware Cyprus is divided into two halves, one half Greek and the other half Turkish, with a UN buffer border between the two factions since their little altercation in 1974. So the arms in those crates are destined for Turkey via Cyprus, and then from Turkey to who knows where, but our best guess would be to Iran. Both Turkey and Iran have a bad habit of arming terrorist groups – Iran is quite open about it, Turkey not so. Now the point is that you may remember a missile attack on the Aramaco fuel depot in Jeddah a couple of years ago?'

I nodded, I remembered it vaguely. An oil storage plant was hit by missiles and blown up, oil prices shot up but the Saudis had it back on stream pretty quickly.

Woodward continued. 'The missiles came from Yemen, fired by the Houthi rebels. Not of general knowledge is that the missiles were British made; and when that was confirmed the Saudis went bloody mad because we are signed up to the UN Covenant on who you can sell arms to and who you can't, selling to Yemen is strictly forbidden. The markings also showed that those missiles were bought from a UK arms manufacturer and the paperwork trail leads from them to Rambart, with the final destination being India. Those missiles obviously didn't go to India, they went to the Houthi via Cyprus, Turkey and Iran. If we pull Rambart in he will have his back well covered, and no doubt have the proper documents from India listing their receipt of the missiles; money buys anything in India, especially from Government officials, so no point in going down that road. However, now we know the route his clandestine missiles take we can be with the ones from the Purley warehouse all the way to their *real* final destination and get the proof we need to shut him down.' He smiled at me. 'Or should I say, *you* can be with them all the way and get the proof we need.' He sat back with that *checkmate* look on his face again.

'I can?' I didn't like the sound of this. 'How?'

'Rambart has his crates booked on a freight flight Heathrow to Lanarca the day after tomorrow. You are booked on a military flight from RAF Wattisham to our base in Akrotiri, Cyprus tomorrow afternoon. Flight leaves 2pm – have whichever passport you are using at present and don't miss it.'

'And what do I do in Cyprus?'

'You follow the crates to their destination, you get proof Rambart is breaking international law and shipping them to Turkey, and then destroy them'

'Destroy armed missiles?' That sounded a bit dodgy to me.

'Yes, of course – can't have them being used, can we.'

'And just how do I destroy them?'

'Oh no doubt you'll find a way – as long as you don't launch the damn things against a friendly power, I really don't care.' He rose and buttoned his coat. 'Have fun, Nevis – and of course if anything goes wrong we will deny all knowledge of you and the operation. Turkish jails have a reputation for being rather insanitary, so do take care.' He gave me a curt nod and left.

My mobile buzzed. It was Gold.

'Was that Woodward?'

'Yes.'

'Good, I hung around to get a look at him so I know him in future. He had two shadows.' The top people in the security networks never go anywhere without a couple of bodyguards along for the ride.

'How do you fancy a few days in Cyprus?'

'Cyprus?'

'Yes, apparently that's where Rambart's crates are going and my job is to follow them from there to establish their final destination and destroy them.'

'So how do I fit in?'

'I want you to follow me, watch my back. I'm dispensable and I'm too young to die in some far Eastern cesspit jail. I'm on an RAF flight to the British base at Akrotiri tomorrow afternoon – the crates are being flown out to Larnarca the next day.'

'All a bit of a rush, isn't it?'

'Can you manage it?'

'Of course I can. I'll give you a bell in Cyprus.'

'Don't forget your sunscreen.'

The line cut off.

That's what I love about Gold, no if and buts – whatever I throw at her she can handle. Nobody I would rather have in my corner.

****

CHAPTER 11

The flight was boring, Looking down at clouds is very soothing but after a while very boring. I was the only passenger on a freight plane full of military supplies. My mood lightened as the clouds dispersed and Cyprus appeared below us drenched in sunshine sitting in the middle of the deep blue Mediterranean. At the Akrotiri base I had assumed I would be met by somebody and given a room. I was, that somebody was a young Lieutenant Commander. He was waiting at the foot of the steps as I came down from the plane, my small rucksack of essentials over my shoulder.

'Mr Nevis?'

'That's me.'

'Lieutenant Commander Jones.' He introduced himself, saluted and shook my hand. 'I'm your local lead partner on this mission, sir.'

A Lieutenant Commander, really? He looked about twenty four – I thought that senior ranks were older? Mind you, James Bond was a Commander in the books and he wasn't very old either, so I must be wrong. Jones was in dark blue shirt and trousers, very informal; he looked very fit and sported a tight one-inch crew cut that accentuated his sharp features. I thought he was probably SBS – most UK military bases on coastlines have an SBS unit woven in.

'Any more luggage, sir?'

'No, everything I need is in here.' I tapped my rucksack. Inside it was a change of underwear, fresh socks, a razor, lockpicks, eight-inch double edge knife in leather sheath and my Walther PPK, plus a box of a hundred bullets. 'And my name is Nevis. Don't call me sir.' I hate any deference.

He smiled. 'Okay, Nevis. I'm Jones.'

'Nice to meet you, Jones.'

He walked me over to a three-story barrack block and saw me into my room on the second floor. Small, compact, bed, shower, wardrobe, table and chair – who could ask for more? Jones brought me up to speed.

'The crates arrive in Larnaca tomorrow – I have eyes on them at the airport and expect them to be classed as Turkish-Cypriot military supplies, so they won't be stopped at Customs and will be taken by armed convoy through the UN buffer zone, up to the border and into one of the Turkish side's border posts. Those posts are pretty big military bases and the crates will probably be opened and checked there and then sent on to one of their ports in Famagusta Bay –probably Trikomo as that's where most of their naval operations work from. Then it's over the Med and into Turkey, probably landing at İskenderun which is a major port and naval base. Then who knows?' He shrugged. 'Some terrorist group is waiting for them somewhere, but they are going to be disappointed.'

'They are?'

'My orders are that as soon as we get proof the missiles are in Turkish hands, we destroy them.'

Woodward had said that to me too. That was worrying. Missiles tend to have rather a loud bang and a wide destruction area.

'How?'

'We'll think of something. Anyway, I expect you'd like a shower and some sleep – looks like a busy few days coming up. Restaurant's on the ground floor.'

'Okay, I think I might wander out and find a local place to eat.'

Jones raised his eyebrows. 'I'm afraid you won't. You are not even here officially, and the Turks take great care in checking for new faces at the gates. They have a snapper there twenty-four seven, if you went out your picture would be on the data scanners in Ankara Military HQ within minutes. The restaurant on base is quite good really, but stick to the steak and chips – none of the local stuff, don't want any tummy trouble when we are on the mission.' He laughed and left me.

Jones was right, the steak and chips – plus fried tomatoes and onion rings – was great. Then it was time for sleep. Funny how a flight drains your energy, I didn't need any rocking.

****

Breakfast in the restaurant the next morning was equally as good as the meal the day before; the full English was tempting but knowing I'd have a busy day ahead I just piled in the carbs with numerous rounds of toast and marmalade. I noticed Jones sitting at another table with two other men; all looked as fit as him so I assumed they were his SBS team. He didn't acknowledge me in the restaurant but caught me up outside as I took a wander round.

'The crates come into Larnaca on a three o'clock flight. Get some rest – I'll pick you up at your room at two and we'll get you fitted out.'

Fitted out sounded ominous, I presumed he meant with firearms. I was already getting the adrenalin buzz that concentrates the senses before a job. *What fun Pip,* eh?

I couldn't get anymore sleep so I just rested. I gave Gold a call about midday to see if she was in Cyprus yet. She was.

'I got a flight from Birmingham early this morning, managed to book a room at the Lysithia Hotel – it's about three miles from the base. What's happening?'

I filled her in on the details.

'Okay, I'll get a flight to Turkey then. I have an old friend in Ankara –not a supporter of the current regime. I'll ask him to get a place in İskenderun tied up in case you need a bolt hole.'

'I like your confidence in me.'

'Nothing to do with having confidence in *you*. You're not on your own in this one Ben, but even if you were I'd do exactly the same – you know I would. You pay me to watch your back, so shut up and let me do my job. Make sure you have the button with you too.' She's so officious.

'Okay, wish me luck.'

'Luck doesn't come into it. Preparation and the right tools for the job does, not luck, make sure you have those with you.' See what I mean, so officious. Reminds me of my primary school teacher Mrs Harris.

'Yes, ma'am.'

'Bollocks, and put the button in now.'

Mrs Harris never said 'bollocks'.

Gold ended the call.

The button was a small disc the size of a coat button which had a lithium battery inside that transmitted a location signal for up to a mile and a half – pretty good range for the size of it. Gold could then pick up the signal on an app on her phone and overlay it onto an area map to see exactly where I was. It had come in very useful before; when I got into tight situations and needed a distraction she could arrange one to help get me out. I had a deep cut in the heel of my right service boot that I had cut long ago where the button lived. I prized it out with my knife and inserted a new battery from the four I keep in my rucksack pocket and pushed it back in.

Jones came for me at two and we walked across the runway and apron to the far side of the base and a brick-built single-storey building. Inside reminded me of a quartermaster's store: shelves of various clothing, all black.

Jones pointed to them. 'Kit yourself out, Nevis – your size will be there somewhere. Leave your clothes in one of the trugs.' He pointed to a row of five plastic trugs on the floor against the back wall; two already had civilian clothes in them, all neatly folded too.

Pretty soon we were dressed to kill, literally. The only thing he let me keep were my boots; they were black anyway, with deep sound-resistant rubber soles, and their steel toecaps kicked at force into an assailant's shin would break his tibia – if aimed a couple of feet higher he'd never have children. And, of course, the button was in the heel. Other than that I had a bulletproof back and front vest, a groin protector that resembled a cricketer's box, and a one piece black stab-proof onesie that went over everything and zipped up down the front that had thin titanium shin guards sewn in the legs. I also had supple gloves with steel knuckle covers, a balaclava, head torch, night goggles and a small black rucksack that I put them in, slipping in my gun, Woodward's mobile, and my own phone at the same time.

'The material is stab-proof, but not bulletproof – so you may feel like Superman inside it, but you're not,' Jones warned me. 'Here, clip this to your belt.'

He handed me the comms battery and the headset that plugged into it before pressing numbers into a keypad on a steel cabinet on the back wall. He opened it and took out a Sig P226 pistol and C8 SFW carbine with two magazines, both full, and a box of ammo for the Sig. I filled the Sig magazine and slotted on the DCF magazine, putting the rest into the rucksack. Next out of the cabinet were two bricks of orange coloured Semtex explosive wrapped in greaseproof paper and two timer fuses. You can drop Semtex on the floor and it won't explode, it needs the fuse. One brick and a fuse into my rucksack the other into Jones's.

'That's all you get – hopefully you won't need to use the guns. All the registration marks are filed off, so neither weapon can be traced back to anywhere if you get caught. I expect Woodward told you that as far as the UK is concerned you don't exist – none of us do – but I am reliably informed that you have past experience in this sort of operation.' He smiled knowingly at me. 'Okay, I think we are ready. Sort your comms out,'

I did that and flicked the button on the battery box to on. I could hear Jones as he checked his team.'

'This is Jones. Comms, are we online yet?'

'Comms online.'

Good. Williams, you there?'

'Williams loud and clear.'

'Good. Taylor, you there?'

'Taylor loud and clear.'

'Good.' He looked at me. 'Nevis, you there?'

'Nevis loud and clear.'

'Good. Williams, update.'

'Crates have left by lorry and making towards the border – they are through Pyla in the UN buffer zone heading towards Pergamos. Williams out.'

'Okay, myself and Nevis will take over at Pergamos. Description please, Williams. Jones out.'

'Three HGVs, all deep green, no markings, driver and mate in each. Williams out.'

'Right. Williams, you two lot back off now and make ready for plan B.'

'Will do. Williams out.'

Jones took an internal phone off its base on the wall and stabbed in a number. Somebody must have answered pretty quick. 'Jones here – we are ready.' He looked at me. 'All set?'

'Yes, I like the code names, Taylor, Williams and Jones .'

He laughed. 'They are the top three surnames in the UK, we don't even know what each other's real names are – saves any confusion.'

He opened the door to the building and almost immediately a UN liveried Transit pulled up as close as it could to the door and its side door slid open. Jones jumped in and motioned me to do the same. As soon as I was inside the door was slid shut by a blue beret UN soldier who stepped through from the rear into the front passenger seat as the driver moved us off.

'The UN?' I asked.

'Of course. They are the peacekeeping force out here, and what we are doing is trying to keep the peace, isn't it?' He smiled.

I shrugged and looked out of the one-way tinted side window.

'Anyway,' Jones continued. 'If we had walked across the base dressed like this and taken a British jeep we would have been picked up by satellite and raise concerns in Turkey. A UN van travelling along the UN border on a regular patrol won't.'

I nodded. Who was I to question the logic in that?

****

CHAPTER 12

It was a bumpy ride over an unmade back road to get into the UN buffer zone and then an equally bad road that meandered along between the Greek security fencing; and barbed wire a hundred metres to our left and the Turkish security fencing and barbed wire a hundred metres to our right. Every now and again a watchtower showed above the fence on the Turkish side, but whether they were manned or not, I couldn't tell. Seeing that there hadn't been any real flare-up between the two sides since 1974, I doubted it.

After thirty minutes or so the UN soldier in the passenger seat turned and spoke.

'We are coming up to the forest now, the tree canopy covers the road so you two can jump out here. No watchtowers up here – and Jones, you know where the tunnel is don't you?'

Jones nodded, 'Yes.'

The tunnel? This was beginning to sound like a World War Two prison camp escape film.

A couple of minutes later the tree canopy covered the road sheltering it from prying drones, the van pulled up and passenger jumped out and slid the side door open. We jumped out and I followed Jones into the undergrowth towards the Turkish side, hearing the door slide shut behind us and the van drive off. Twenty metres into the bush Jones hit the ground and I copied and lay twelve feet to his right. All was quiet.

'Give it ten minutes – they fly drones, so if we were seen they should have a patrol up here by then. We'll be able to hear their vehicles if they do.'

The wait gave me time to assess my position. I was about to go uninvited into Turkish military territory, and they aren't exactly known for their adherence to human rights; I was to find and destroy some missiles, and if Nicholas Rambart shows up kill him to claim my eight hundred grand bounty from his wife. Easy peasy – be back in time for breakfast, eh? No way.

Time to move.

'Okay, this way.' Jones led as we ducked our way through the undergrowth until he stopped, sank to his knees and brushed away the dead leaves and twigs on the ground to reveal a large steel ring on a hinge overgrown with grass and weeds. It took Jones a few heaves until the grass gave up and released a metal cover, much the same size as a street manhole which Jones pulled open.

'In you go – you'll need your head torch on.'

I flicked it on and took a tentative step onto the first rungs of a steel ladder leading down the tight entrance. Ten steps later I was at the bottom and saw a tunnel leading off; above me Jones was in and pulled the cover back down, shutting out and light from outside. He joined me at the bottom of the steps.

'I'll lead,' he said, ducking into the tunnel which was square but only about four foot high, meaning we had to crawl on all fours along it. It was pretty basic, not exactly state of the art – just a hole hewn from the solid rock; the only benefit was that it sloped away from us as we crawled along, which meant any rain that had come in had flowed away and the floor was pretty dry. After ten minutes Jones stopped and looked round.

'Take a breather. You okay?'

'I'm fine. how much further?'

'Nearly there. It comes out on a hillside – originally it was dug by the Greek Cypriots who were taken prisoner in the war, only they travelled the other way of course.' He smiled.

'Of course.'

'It comes out on a steep slope in dense undergrowth, so the Turks don't go there and haven't found it. Last bit coming up, ready?'

'Yes.'

At least there wasn't a ladder to climb at the end, just an overgrown open hole that took us a few minutes to hack through and emerge into the undergrowth on the hillside. Obviously the tunnel wasn't in regular use.

We sat there, looking through the foliage down to Famagusta Bay about two miles away; lights were beginning to twinkle as day moved into night.

Jones flicked on his comms. 'Jones to Coms,'

'Comms reading you loud and clear, Jones.'

'Update please, Comms.'

'Comms to Jones, we have satellite coverage of the lorries – they have passed Prastio and turned right at Lefkoniko, heading towards Trikomo or maybe Bogaz. Both those places have docks, but Trikomo is clear at present and Bogaz has two freighters moored dockside and some activity loading one of them.'

'Thank you, Comms. Looks like Bogaz then. Williams, are you hearing this?'

'Williams to Jones. Yes, got that.'

'Okay, good. Move to three miles offshore within twenty minutes of Bogaz.'

'Williams, will do.'

'Jones over and out.' He turned to me, 'Right, we need some transport to get us to Bogaz.'

I was a little confused. 'Why are we going this way when a fast skiff from the base could get us there in half an hour?'

Jones laughed. 'You're right, it could – but a fast skiff leaving the base and going towards Bogaz would be picked up by the Turks' radar and have three Turkish fast skiffs for company within a couple of miles. Turkey claims sovereign rights over a three-mile coastal water zone around north Cyprus; it's disputed of course, but they tend to shoot first and ask questions afterwards. Coming overland is the best option of arriving unobserved.'

We moved at a pretty fast pace down the slope towards the lights, and pretty soon we hit the Prastio road and followed it, keeping a good fifty metres off to the side of it, sheltered by the trees and bushes. After a mile we stopped and ducked down; a hundred metres in front of us a truck stop in a wide parking area beside the road shone out its lights into the now total darkness, illuminating the vehicles waiting as their owners took a break inside. It was busy, the vehicles ranging from lorries to motorbikes; the customers were coming and going from inside the building from where we could hear a general hubbub of noise, music and laughter. The woodland gave us cover right up to the back row of parked cars furthest from the building.

Jones motioned towards a Lexus which was furthest from the building and nearest to us. We moved up beside it; I knelt behind and aimed my C8 carbine at the truck stop door as Jones used the stock of his to smash the driver side rear passenger window, before reaching through to open the driver's door, slip inside, smash the thin plastic covering the steering column, yank out the wires either side of the ignition switch and touch the bare ends together to start the engine. Reaching across he opened the passenger door for me to get in and we were off out of the car park and on the road to Lefkonico where we turned right towards Bagaz. Most of the traffic was military so we didn't want to stay with the Lexus for too long as its ID would be sent over the airwaves quite quickly after the theft was reported.

Bagaz is an old Cypriot village that has re-invented itself as big seaside resort; skyscraper hotels adorn the front promenade looking out over the bay and modern villas and apartment blocks surround them, with the old town and dock a little further up the coast towards us. At this time of year it was dead, except for the locals and the military from a small base nearby. As we approached it Jones slowed down and took a right turn into a small lane off the main road.

'You know the way. Been here before?' I asked.

'No, just want to dump this car away from the main area – don't want it found in the town. Hopefully if they find it they'll think it was just kids having a joyride.'

The lane wound through thick forest; every now and again a shaft of moonlight fought its way through the canopy and lit the bumpy lane ahead of us which soon petered out and came to an end at a wooden five bar gate. I could see the ocean in front of us but no beach, must be a cliff edge. We got out, climbed the gate and walked across a fifty metre grassed area that ended at the edge of a steep cliff with the sea smashing against it far below.

'Just the job,' Jones smiled at me. 'Hold the gate open whilst I bring the car through.'

We went back to the gate and I did as he said and watched as he drove the car slowly towards the edge, jumping out a few metres before it nosedived over. I remember doing that on the South Downs a long time back with a Ford Consul that had two bodies in the boot and the bloody thing sticking on the edge, with the front over it and the back on the ground. Nowadays with four-wheel drive, no problem – if it's in gear the back wheels push it over.

We started walking along the cliff top towards the old town and the dock. The moon was giving us enough light to see the way forward, but we took the precaution of putting our night vision glasses on, just in case – a bit cumbersome, but we'd see someone before they saw us. The cliff top began to give way to the narrow pebbled streets of the old town with rows of small two-storey stone built farm worker houses either side, three to a row with a narrow alleyway between each block. Their windows had the wooden shutters closed; slits of light shone through from some, and every now and again laughter and raised voices could be heard from inside.

A choice had to be made: carry on along the streets to the dock, or skirt round the back where their backyards gave way to a wide shingle beach. Trouble was, if they had dogs they would be tethered round the back and would probably bark their heads off at us. The streets weren't lit, so we took a chance that nobody would be about at that time of night and carried on.

Big mistake. We should have taken our chances with the dogs. An open army jeep swung into the narrow road from a cross roads fifty metres further on, headlights blazing, and caught us in the glare. I wasn't even thinking that they'd patrol this area, but with the ultra nationalist Turkish Grey Wolves Islamic terrorist group very active in north Cyprus with strikes against the army we maybe should have factored that into our thoughts. We had the advantage that they would be confused seeing two black-clad and armed men in their lights and had to stop and get their guns out; ours were slung over our shoulders and primed to go.

I swung my carbine up and loosed off a few rounds on automatic, taking out the headlights. Jones stepped across the narrow street to make a separate target and knelt on one knee as he did the same, his shots disintegrating the windscreen and driver's head. Out of control, the jeep careered into the nearest house as I took care of the remaining two occupants. Lights were going on and doors opening all along the street as people came out to see what was happening. I nodded to Jones to follow me and ran down the nearest alley – the chained dogs were already barking so no need to be careful now as we ran towards the sea with the slope of the land giving some cover from behind. Once below the sightline from the houses we struck out towards the dock area which was lit up about a mile and a half further on. Behind us we could hear sirens and shouting; the upside was that the authorities would no doubt think this was a Grey Wolves random attack, and not be thinking it was from outside the area and that maybe the docks were the target

'Into the water,' I shouted to Jones who was ten metres in front. 'They'll have dogs.'

He raised an arm in agreement and we ran down into the surf, which slowed us down but would lose our scent. After what must have been a mile we halted and took a rest. Looking back at the old village we could see searchers' lights were all over the shore and a line of them coming our way. It was an obvious choice for the pursuers if they thought we were Grey Wolves, we would be going towards the town and a safe house, so why would we go the other way into bracken and forest where dogs would soon find us? So we had to keep going, as no doubt they'd be sending troops down onto the beach all the way along towards the dock; it was just a matter of being ahead of them and getting into some decent cover.

My legs were feeling tired from running in water but the adrenalin had kicked in and we hurried on. Then we heard it – the unmistakable whirring of helicopter blades. It was coming from the dock area, its searchlight scanning the beach. We turned up the slope inland, over a small perimeter wall and into a beach hotel garden. It was pretty open ground and deserted being out of season, but there wasn't enough time to make it across the grounds to the building itself before the helicopter searchlight would pick us up.

'The deckchairs!' I shouted to Jones. I'd seen two piles of stacked deckchairs over by the pool.

We ran to them and squeezed in between the piles, reaching up to pull the top ones over the gap we stood in – if the 'copter saw us we were sitting ducks. He swept his searchlight over the grounds for what seemed an eternity before making off further along the beach.

We didn't hang about and started off towards the lights of the dockside, again keeping below the sightline of the beach.

The end of the concrete dock came into view, wide unlit concrete steps leading up to it from the beach. We crept up and peeped over onto the apron. Nothing happening this end;

there were the two big freighters comms had mentioned tied up alongside about a hundred metres further along. All the activity seemed to be around the furthest one, which was steel grey and had Turkish Navy markings; an overhead crane was lifting on pallets with what looked like Rambart's crates strapped to them. The lifeboats hanging on the freighter's side swung slightly on their gantries as the crates were lowered into the hold, causing the boat to rock a little. The three green HGVs were parked with their back doors open facing the ship. I took a good look through the telescopic lens of the CF8 – yes, they were Rambart's crates. On our left and all the way along the back of the dock apron ship containers were stacked three high in lanes. I motioned Jones to follow and made for the first lane. We worked our way along until we were opposite the ship being loaded and could watch proceedings through the gaps between the containers.

'See the crates being loaded on?' I asked Jones.

'Yes.'

'They are the target. They mustn't reach Turkey.'

'Okay, how do you want to play it – blow the whole lot up?'

'Yes, but not here. I want to get onboard and sink her once outside the three-mile limit. The blame will be hung on the USA or a host of Middle Eastern Countries taking revenge for the attack on the Saudi oil tanks in Jeddah.'

'Did Turkey do that?'

'No, the Houthis did it. But the missiles came in through Turkey – they act as a middleman. These missiles might not be going to Yemen, but wherever they are going it's not good news.'

Jones nodded. 'Okay, so we have to get onboard then.'

'Should be easy once the crates are onboard. The dockers will want to get off home and that only leaves the ship's crew, and that won't be many – just a couple in the engine room and the master and two others in the wheelhouse. It's a freighter, not a warship.'

It was a good half hour before the crane driver climbed down the steel ladder from his cage. I shook Jones who had managed to drop off sitting next to me. We watched as the dock crew slammed the HGV doors shut and walked off *en masse* towards the main entrance at the far end of the dock. We took off our rucksacks and edged through the small gap between the containers towards the lit dockside with me in front. Voices! We froze as three people crossed my line of vision and stopped at the foot of the gangplank; they shook hands and two started off up the gangplank. The one in front turned to give a last wave to the man left on the dockside – the face was unmistakeable. What was Eve Rambart doing onboard a freighter with missiles heading for Turkey? I took a quick picture on Woodward's phone, making sure the flash was off, and sent it. I think there was enough light from the dock lights to show who it was,

****

CHAPTER 13

People often query my bill for the time charged on a job – they forget how many hours the PI spends sitting, watching and waiting for the mark to move. And so it was with this caper. I got over my surprise of seeing Eve Rambart go onboard the freighter and we stayed still, giving her and the goon with her time to settle in. The Captain, or somebody with a peaked officer-type hat, had welcomed her on deck and gone with her inside out of view. Freighters usually have a couple of extra crew cabins, so perhaps she was making herself comfortable in one of those for the trip.

It was forty minutes before the one with the peaked cap re-emerged onto the deck gangway, made his way along it for three-quarters of the ship's length and then up some steps to the large wheelhouse that spanned the breadth of the ship. Now was our chance. We emerged from the gap and walked across to the gangplank as though we should be there; sometimes hiding in plain sight works, although this time there probably wasn't anybody to see us and wonder who we were, but you never know. Once onboard Jones followed me along the gangway away from the wheelhouse to the far stern of the ship, where we hid behind a large anchor chain windlass which sheltered us from view.

Before long activity on the deck and dock pointed towards an imminent departure. The mooring ropes were slipped off their dock moorings and hauled up and the heavy throb of the diesels starting up shook the deck as they fought the water to turn the giant propellers. The dockside slipped away behind us as we edged out into the main breakwater bay, past the end of that with its flashing red warning light and into the Med. We gave it another ten minutes for everything in the wheelhouse and engine room to settle down; the officers and engineers would probably settle back with a drink and relax, with everything on autopilot. Nothing to do now until we were well clear of coastal waters. Jones sat and I watched Cyprus fade into the far horizon as daylight began to break.

'You think we are in international waters yet?' I asked after a while.

He pulled a mobile from his shin pocket and turned it on, then using his thumb to page through various apps found the one he was after. It was a map of the Mediterranean, showing us a flashing red dot in the middle of it off the far tip of Cyprus.

'Looks like we are, but better give it another thirty minutes to make sure.'

'Wake me up then.' I settled back and closed my eyes; he'd grabbed forty winks at the dock, so my turn now.

In what seemed only a minute later a jab in the arm woke me up from my slumber.

'We're in international waters now,' said Jones. 'Let's go.'

I slung the carbine round to my back, pulled out the Sig and took off the safety; Jones had done the same. Then I pulled down my balaclava and followed him along the side gangway and we took up position either side of the door Eve Rambart had gone through. It was solid – no window – so I turned the handle slowly and pushed it open. Inside was a corridor that had doors off it and at the end an opening in the floor with a steel staircase leading down into it. The cover to close off the staircase was propped open and the deep thudding noise of pistons turning the drive shaft to the ship's propeller somewhere below us came up the well of the staircase, together with a blast of heat; the engine room was down there.

I set foot on the stair rungs and went down slowly my Sig in my hand, looking around as I went. The stairs led down directly into the engine room, and the noise became deafening as I reached the floor level. Two big steel turbines hid the stairs from the rest of the engine room, I beckoned Jones down and he joined me. The heat was quite suffocating, which I assumed was why the stair cover was open. Peeping round the turbines I could see three men: one was sitting at a table with bottles of drink on it reading a paper, the other two were standing in front of an array of gauges on the back wall checking pressures and taking readings. Their naval insignia jackets and caps were hung on wall hooks and their three rifles were leaning against the wall.

I raised two fingers to Jones and pointed to the two standing – I'll take them. He nodded and we walked out from behind the turbines and were within twelve feet before they noticed us and made for their rifles – well, how can you miss from that distance? The first shot from my Sig was already aimed at the back of one man's head and he crumpled to the ground as it sped through his brain and left via his forehead; my second target was so shocked and surprised to see us he couldn't move, which allowed me time to make sure my second shot had the same effect on him, only going in at the front and out the back. Jones's target had suffered the same quick death. No way would the shots have been heard above the engine noise, so we were quite relaxed – nobody would come running.

Yeah, I know what you are thinking – we just killed three men, maybe three husbands, or dads, or brothers. I know, but that's what I do – not often, and without people like me you wouldn't sleep so soundly at night, would you? You have to remember these are military people, who signed up knowing the risks; these are the bad guys who are transporting live missiles to an enemy who will pass them on to some other enemy, who will probably aim them at a busy public target to cause the most damage and kill maybe a hundred or so of the good guys. You want to live in a failed state run by warring warlords? Okay, disband MI5 and 6 and that's what you'll get, believe me.

Taking off our rucksacks we pulled out the slabs of Semtex and peeled off their greaseproof wrappers. There was an obvious place to set an explosion for the maximum result, and that was where the large driveshafts went through the ship's hull to the propellers. Semtex is very malleable and like playing with plasticine, so I was easily able to mould around the thick eighteen-inch rubber seals where the drive shaft went through the hull. As I was working at that, Jones took out the timers and set them for thirty minutes. I checked my watch – I wasn't going to be anywhere near this ship when that lot went off. He pushed the timers into the

Semtex, and I could see their LEDs flashing red as the seconds ticked by. Dangerous things, timers; basically they ticked away for thirty minutes or whatever length of time you set them for, and then a small battery sent an electric shock through a small amount of magnesium which flared up, exploding a small amount of Semtex or dynamite that in turn exploded the main charge. Simple, effective and deadly.

We had thirty minutes to get off that ship. When the Semtex and timers were all set we dragged the bodies out of sight and went carefully back up the staircase. I poked my head up and saw the corridor was clear before we hauled ourselves up into it. We slowly lowered the heavy steel cover to close the opening and I saw a padlock that, looking at its size, was obviously for fastening the cover shut when the ship was laid up, as it fitted the large hasp welded on the cover exactly. I pushed it through and shut it, putting the key in my pocket.

We made our way swiftly back outside to the stern and settled in behind the anchor chain windlass again, checking in front and behind as we went. It had begun to rain when we were below and was steadily getting worse and developing into a storm. Lightning was arching over the sky above us which had grown dark and threatening and the wind was whipping up the waves and starting to rock the freighter.

Jones pulled his radio from his rucksack and switched it on.

'Jones to Williams, come in.'

There was a short break before he got a reply.

'Williams here, sir. Go ahead, you're loud and clear.'

'Jones to Williams, we are ready to embark ASAP. What's your ETA?'

'Williams to Jones, we are half a mile on your starboard side. With you in ten.'

'Jones to Williams, okay. We are at the stern and will be ready. Jones out.'

I raised myself a little and looked over the broad railings on the starboard side. I couldn't see any boat coming our way; in fact I couldn't see much at all as the rain lashed in at me and the wind tore off the top of the waves and hurled them over the railing.

'Don't bother looking, you won't see them coming.' Jones had to shout above the storm now, 'They're on a stealth boat, low in the water and very fast – or to give it its proper name, an FB Mil-50P. Any the wiser?' he asked and was laughing. He likes laughing, does Jones – I wonder if it was to compensate for any fear he was feeling in this situation? I'd read somewhere that people sometimes do that.

'No, just so long as it's fast and gets us away from here before that Semtex goes up,' I shouted back above the noise of the storm and driving rain which was running down my face.

Jones laughed again. 'No problem. Come on, we need to get as near to the back of the ship as we can – Williams will approach from behind. If they've got radar on in the wheelhouse he won't show much of a picture; the FBs are built of anti-radar material except for the engines, but we still need to get away fast.'

'Has he been tracking us all the way then?'

'Not all the way – he waited outside the three-mile zone and has been with us since then.'

'You didn't say.'

'How else do you think we'll get back to base when the ship goes down, swim?' Another laugh.

We crawled to the back of the ship, staying below any sightline from the rest of it and waited, getting more and more wet. The third time I checked my watch annoyed Jones.

'Don't panic, Nevis. We will be away before the big bang.'

‘I bloody hope so.’

His radio cracked into action.

‘Williams to Jones.’

I thought all we need now is Williams to say his engine has failed, but he didn’t.

‘Go ahead, Williams.’

‘We are right below you, sir.’

We both knelt up and peered over the stern railing. Below in the churning water caused by the storm and the propeller blades six foot below the surface, we could see Williams standing in the bow of what looked like a medium-sized speedboat to me; he held what looked like a gun, but the barrel was far too wide for that. Jones gave him the thumbs up and pulled me back down to the deck.

‘Cover your head with your arms, he’s firing a rope up to us.’

So that was what Williams was holding: a bloody big air gun.

A small metal grappling hook only about three inches in length with three hooks came sailing high over the railing and clattered to the deck a few feet in front of us. Jones retrieved it and starting pulling on the monofilament nylon line attached to it, which soon gave way to a decent size climbing rope. I helped him pull a few yards over the railing until we had enough of a length to tie it in a reef knot around one of the big steel links of the anchor chain.

'Over you go.' Jones indicated I should climb over the railing and go down the rope. It looked a long way down, about eighty feet on a wet swinging rope to a small boat bouncing in the propeller wake on a stormy sea – nice. I climbed over, took hold of the rope with both hands, twisted my right foot round it and using my left as a brake I abseiled down in fits and starts until Williams's welcoming hands pulled me onboard the bouncing skiff.

'Get down and put a safety belt on,' he shouted above the noise of the churning water. In the well of the boat Taylor was handling the big double engines at the back, keeping her tight against the ship's hull as Jones clambered over and started down. Taylor tapped me on the shoulder and pointed to a safety harness, basically a belt attached to the inside of the boat that went round my waist and clicked together. Jones joined us and fell beside me, clicking on his belt as Taylor swung the boat to the right and we sped away from the ship at warp speed. I looked at my watch and pointed at the face, showing it to Jones.

'Three minutes!'

Jones nodded and shouted above the noise to Taylor. 'Give it all you've you got, she goes up in three.'

The big engines sounded a deep roar as Taylor hit the fuel injector and opened them up full. I found myself holding onto the safety belt as the boat bumped across the stormy waves that were getting bigger by the minute as the storm set in.

We were about a quarter of a mile from the ship when we saw it first and then heard it – a sheet of red flame like a giant Roman candle shot up into the air from the rear half of the ship, and a dull thud followed it.

'That's the fuel tanks,' Jones shouted.

Taylor cut the engines and we watched as the rest of the ship was engulfed in flame, and the air filled with the noise of continuing explosions as the armaments in the crates exploded. The missiles wouldn't explode as modern missiles are triggered by what's called a proximity fuse, which is programmed to detonate the payload when the missile reaches a pre-determined distance from the target; the ones on the freighter wouldn't have been programmed and they would be bent and battered by the explosions around them, dropping to the sea floor with the remains of the freighter as it sank as it surely would. Time to send Woodward an update, I took out his phone and sent a picture, probably out of focus through the storm but he should realise what it was and be happy.

Williams was watching the freighter through night vision binoculars.

'Somebody's made it away,' he said, passing the glasses to Jones. 'Do we go after them and finish the job?'

Jones looked and then turned to me. 'It's the lady you recognised at the dock and one other. Here, take a look.'

He was right – Eve Rambart was sitting in a lifeboat speeding away from the burning ship; I could only see one other person with her and he was at the back steering it. They were going away from us, heading towards the Turkish coast.

'You want to chase them?' shouted Taylor, starting the engines again.

Jones had taken the glasses back and was looking towards the coast.

'If we do we'll have company – there's a small flotilla of naval craft on their way.' He passed the glasses back to me and I could see what he was talking about. Fast small boats were bouncing over the waves towards the stricken ship, blue lights flashing, and every now and again the sound of sirens could be heard filtering through the storm to us. It would be suicidal to get mixed up in a firefight with them – we'd be well outnumbered. I swung the glasses right and looked towards the shore which was dark, overgrown with scrub and looked forbidding, then further right where the lights of Latakia could be seen. One thing was for sure, I had to go after Eve Rambart – had she been fooling us all along? She was only on the ship for one reason, delivering the missiles, and she wouldn't have been there if they were a shipment from her husband. Putting two and two together was easy: *she* was the arms dealer putting these deadly weapons into Turkey and Iran, not Nicholas. Could be she'd been doing it for years, and the previous two husbands had found out and had to be killed? Had Nicholas found out too and was that why he wanted her killed and vice versa why she wanted him killed? She was stepping on his toes, threatening his business with her own, she had to go. Could be, but there was only one way to find out.

'Put me ashore over there.' I pointed to the nearest land which was to the left of Latakia.

'Syrian territory,' shouted Jones. 'No way, Nevis – they have patrols all along that shore and the sea and beaches are mined. You'd be lucky to last five minutes.'

'I've got to find out who's shipping those missiles in for definite. Can you get me ashore anywhere along there?'

Jones looked at Taylor who shrugged. 'Yes, I can get in to the shore on the Turkish side down from Antakya, but whether I'd get out again without being seen is doubtful – there are lots of patrols in that area. It's near to the Turkey-Syria border, and both are a bit trigger-happy since Idlib was bombed and half a million refugees stormed the border. There is a sand bank – the sea is fairly shallow for about two hundred metres out from the beach, but there's no cover. I've landed ops there before '

'Good.' That gave me a lift.

'But none of them ever made the return pick-up time.' Taylor gave me a smile and raised his eyebrows, asking the unspoken question *'are you sure?'*.

I didn't have a choice; I had to confirm it was Eve Rambart shipping the missiles. 'Well, there's always a first time.'

Taylor looked at Jones for orders.

Jones nodded. 'Let's go for it.'

Taylor swung the boat round towards the shore and we headed in, keeping an eye on the boats heading for the burning ship which was now just a very big flaming superstructure floating on the sea, with the occasional explosion of gas bottles and onboard armaments adding to the display.

As we got to within two hundred yards of the shore, myself Jones and Williams scanned it with night vision binoculars, looking for military patrols or any other movement. It seemed all quiet. Taylor brought us in on idle speed to keep the noise down and we all kept low in the boat; Williams had his AK-47 on night vision mode trained on the dark undergrowth above the beach. The dark storm and lashing rain whipping up the waves gave us good cover in such a low profile boat, and I doubt whether anybody would be able to hear us even at full throttle above the noise of the storm. The waves got smaller as we neared the beach until they flattened out over the sandbank.

'Right – listen, Nevis.' Jones eased next to me and shouted above the storm into my ear. 'We will be back for you here at one o'clock in the morning every night for the next seven, okay? After that, you're on your own. Flash a light – three short and one long.' He patted my back. 'Good luck, off you go.'

****

CHAPTER 14

I swung myself over the side and dropped into the sea, hoping Taylor had got the depth right; he had, my feet touched the bottom with the water up to my chest. I let go of the boat and pushed against the sea towards the shore. Taylor waited until I was a good twenty metres away before I heard him increase the throttle slightly, and looking back I could see the FB intermittently between the waves making its way back out to sea, heading left to give the activity around the blazing ship a wide berth. I took no chances, stooping down so only my head was above the water and waited, counting to sixty just in case there was any activity on the shore or coming down from the scrub it led up to. Nothing – no Turkish Special Services Marines appearing out of the scrub to turn me into fish food.

I waded forward and left the water onto the beach where I knelt to get my bearings and relax for a moment – all good so far. That was until I saw headlights moving behind the scrub a good quarter mile away in front of me. The land sloped slightly upwards and the lights were going right to left – there must be a road; they stopped briefly and then continued out of sight along the road. Good, a road would make travel a lot easier than stumbling through thick undergrowth.

I got to my feet and moved up off the beach into the scrub, finding a tree to stand behind and drip dry. I checked my rifle and pistol; they were SBS issue, well-greased so the salt-laden sea water wouldn't stop them operating, but I took no chances with the bullets, emptying out the ones in the magazines and replacing them with dry ones from my rucksack. The black onesie was not only stab-proof but waterproof as well, with tight Velcro seals around the neck, wrists, ankles and pockets that had kept my undergarments dry, so when it was fairly drip dry I felt comfortable inside it. I needed to be able to pinpoint this place if I was going to get back here and rendezvous with Jones for the journey back to Cyprus so I used the location app on my mobile and took a reading before making my way slowly up towards the road, fighting against the thick scrub and undergrowth tendrils which had other ideas.

From the side of the road I could see the lights of Antakya further down it – a long way further down it – and started a slow run towards them; run a hundred yards and then take a breather, then another hundred, take a breather, and so on. I had to dive into the bushes a few times when a car came past either way; I could see their lights a good way off and was well-hidden as they passed. They were all military vehicles, which was to be expected being so close to the border. Despite the breathers every hundred yards the fatigue still built up in my legs, and after about a mile I sat down and rested.

That was a mistake.

'Hareket etmeyi!'

A voice shouted at me from close by.

'Ellerini kaldır!'

I looked to my right from where I was sitting and in the gloom a Turkish soldier had me covered with his rifle; he was in camouflage clothing and his face was blacked out. I don't speak Turkish but guessed what he was telling me to do and raised my arms. He moved his rifle barrel up and down, signifying I was to stand, which I did; he kicked my rifle which was on the ground away from me, and waved his rifle sideways for me to go out of the scrub onto the road with him behind me. How long had he been on my trail? I thought back to when I was on the beach and had seen vehicle lights stop on the road and then move off again. Had they spotted me then and dropped him off to track me? Why wait until now? Probably because I was getting near the town. I waited, expecting to hear him make a radio call for a jeep to come and collect me. My mind was now concentrating on turning the tables on him before that jeep arrived; if not, then incarceration in a filthy Turkish prison compound looked very likely.

I heard a moan behind me and turned to see the soldier drop his rifle and sink to the ground, blood spurting from his neck where his throat was cut. Behind him a figure in much the same gear as me stood holding a large knife which glinted in the moonlight.

'He's been following you since you landed,' Gold said in a matter of fact way, turning up her balaclava. 'Give me a hand to put him out of sight.'

She bent and grabbed the soldier's legs. I thought it best to just do as she said and ask questions afterwards. We lifted the body through the scrub and trees for fifty yards off the road and dumped it. She unfastened his radio from his belt, took the batteries out and threw them far into the woods. I threw the rifle even further in, swinging it round me and away like an Olympic hammer thrower.

'How did you know?' I asked.

'You've a radio button in your heel, or have you forgotten that?' she laughed.

I had forgotten that.

'We picked you up about half a mile offshore and tracked you to the beach. Luckily I was already waiting for you in the woods beside the road when his patrol came through and saw you, and he started following.'

'What about the rest of his patrol?'

'They'll be further down the road at the outskirts of the city waiting, hoping you were meeting some insurgents and then they'd get the lot. Anyway, enough about him – let's get you sorted out.' She spoke Turkish into a radio which was answered also in Turkish.

A few minutes later a van pulled up – an old battered van, no lights and just a driver; he was late middle-age, in rough clothing and an old peaked cap, and didn't speak. Gold opened the rear doors and pulled out a change of clothing for both of us. She had it all planned – why was I not surprised? Because it's Gold; nothing left to chance, ever. I noticed some building materials inside, so that was our cover; in a few minutes we were both just ordinary Turkish construction workers. Our onesies disappeared into the rucksack and Gold wrapped on a hijab. We both crammed onto the one threadbare passenger seat and started on our way towards the city of Antakya.

****

The early morning light was filtering through the dawn mist as we drove into Antakya; the streetlights were still on and early traffic starting to move around. I looked out to the bay, a good ten miles away on our left now – no activity – and looking out further I expected to see a smouldering skeleton of the ship, but there was nothing; she must have sunk – well, that was the plan after all. Woodward said not to let the missiles reach Turkey, and they hadn't. But seeing Eve Rambart board the ship and escape the inferno had added a chapter to the plan; now I had to find and kill her, seeing as she was obviously the one organising the illegal arms sales. And, of course, I also had my eyes on a million quid bounty from hubby. Mercenary, me? But of course.

We were in the old part of Antakya and pulled up outside a cafe half full of workers having their breakfast. A rickety table at the back had a scrawled note on it: *Saklı –dır*. Gold saw me look at it and provided the answer to my unasked question. 'Reserved.'

No sooner had we sat than the waiter, or maybe the owner, was at our side: plump, middle-aged, unshaven and wearing a striped apron that really needed to go in the wash. Gold held up three fingers and he was gone.

'This is Ajdin.' She introduced our driver who smiled and nodded. 'Ajdin and I go back a long way.'

I didn't ask questions; I knew Gold had been operating inside Turkey when Turkey supported ISIS, and she had probably had some input into the PKK and Armenian Front. But that was none of my business, I don't ask questions – if you don't know things then they can't be forced out of you by torture or drugs. The current Erdoğan regime in Turkey has a lot of internal enemies and had put down a military coup a few years back, so whether Ajdin was still involved wasn't my concern – not my contact, and in this business you have your own contacts and stay away from other people's. Although I never had any direct contacts in the Middle East, Gold would have had many in her time with Mossad. Perhaps Ajdin was one of those.

The breakfast was served up quickly and was delicious – a dish of *menemem* with Turkish bread, *sucuk* and *pastırma*, followed by fruit jam, honey and black tea. Most of my English friends think Turks survive on doner kebabs – they don't, and certainly not on the crap bone scrapings mixed with pulverised offal called doner kebab that we get in the UK. We ate in silence; sometimes you get a meal and just want to take time and fully enjoy it – this was one such meal. Nothing out of the ordinary to a Turkish worker, but after the day and night I'd just had it was a joy.

'Okay, let's go,' Gold gave the order when we had finished. Ajdin paid the bill and as we left the cafe and went back to the van.

'What's the plan then?' I asked as Gold and I crammed back into the passenger seat and Ajdin started the engine and we moved off.

'Sleep, that's the plan, Ben – a good long sleep. I've done some research and we are going to have to have our wits about us for what's in store, so first you get some shut-eye.'

I must admit I could fall asleep without much rocking; it had been a mentally and physically exhausting two days since I left the base.

Ajdin drove us out of the town and through a couple of small villages before taking to unmade roads and tracks for a mile or so before pulling up at a very palatial-looking building set in its own compound with several armed guards on patrol.

'I'm impressed, is this your holiday home?' I joked at Gold.

'No, couldn't afford this – even Turkey has its rich entrepreneurs. The one who owns this also has a dislike for the Erdoğan regime and is only too happy to quietly aid others of the same persuasion. Don't talk to anybody, and no pictures.'

A housemaid met us at the door, nothing was said as she led us through the marble tiled ground floor and out to an open compound at the back of the house, then across it to a separate building set on its own. It looked like a stable on the outside but inside it was a large single room that reminded me of an American motel: bed, shower, table, chairs and TV. The guest room for guests you can't acknowledge? Probably.

Gold stood in the doorway as I tried the bed for softness; it was hard, but no matter – it was a bed.

'Sleep well. There'll be a man just outside, so don't wander – just sleep. I have a couple of things to do and then I'll be back later.'

She shut the door and to be honest I don't even remember lying on the bed, but the next thing I knew Gold was shaking me awake.

'Come on, sleeping beauty – time to get planning.'

She had laid out a map of the town on the table. Ajdin had my welfare at heart and had thoughtfully made me a coffee to kick up the adrenalin. I pulled a chair up to the table and sat down.

Gold pointed to an area on the outskirts of the city. 'Military industrial and warehouse area, the place armaments are stored when in transit, so had that lot of missiles on the ship made it this is where they would be.'

'They didn't make it, but by your interest in the place I assume other stuff has?'

'Tons of it, and all neatly stacked in one warehouse ready to be moved on to whichever terrorist group needs it. It's a major distribution hub for illegal ordnance, but the trick is that the warehouse is the store for legal ordnance too so it all looks kosher from outside with genuine Turkish military arms orders being delivered and housed there too, all with the correct paperwork.'

'Clever, hiding in plain sight.'

'Very clever.'

I was getting the picture of where this conversation was going. 'I just need to take out Eve Rambart. Woodward said to stop the missiles getting to their destination and I've done that, the warehouse isn't my concern. I'll text Woodward, give him the co-ordinates and he can call in a missile strike on it.'

'Too late, can't be done – Erdoğan bought the Russian S-400 surface-to-air missile defence system from Putin in 2018 and secured Turkey's airspace. The missiles and ordnance in that warehouse will be going forward to various terrorist groups and have to be stopped. Any hit has to be done over ground.'

'Which means us,' I said, with a degree of resignation.

'No, not us – you.'

How did I know that was coming?

She continued, 'If I get caught they know my history, and being ex-Mossad I'd be hung in an hour.'

'And me?'

'They'd negotiate, a prisoner swap or something.' She dismissed the conversation with a wave of her hand. 'Anyway, we won't get caught because we don't have to go in ourselves; we can't call an air strike but we can get a drone in there – two drones, in fact.'

'Two? Why two?' So this was the plan.

'The warehouse we need to hit has large glass roof skylights; frosted glass so satellites can't see inside, but just plain glass – no reinforcing steel fibres, just plain glass. It's an old building, built in the fifties so security wasn't paramount then. The first drone we send over it is loaded with weights and smashes through the skylight; the second one drops in with an explosive incendiary bomb attached. Our information is that there's enough explosive in that warehouse to blow the place sky high.'

'Sounds good, you got the gear in place?' If it was she had certainly worked hard in the two days she'd been in Turkey.

'All in the back of the van, two drones and a box of explosive. We hit the warehouse tonight.'

'Tonight? What about Rambart? I've unfinished business there.'

'You can catch up with her later – what's important is that those missiles in the warehouse don't move anywhere else. If they go underground to some terrorist organisation we've lost them.' She gave me a hard look. 'Lost them until they rain down on some civilian town or hospital somewhere.'

I didn't argue – she was right, I could kill Rambart at some other time. She picked up a rucksack she'd brought in with her and emptied out the onesies.

We put them on. Showtime!

Showtime was interrupted by the door flying open and two Turkish soldiers with rifles raised rushing in. Taken by surprise, there was nothing we could do except raise our hands as their officer followed them in holding a pistol. He spoke in broken English.

'What have we here then – English spies? Do you think we don't know you are here, eh? You think we Turkish are stupid, eh? You think people don't talk, walls have ears as you English say? People here know what side their bread is buttered, eh Ajdin?' He smiled at Ajdin who lowered his arms.

Gold said the words slowly with a lot of venom in her voice. 'You bastard, Ajdin. You fucking bastard.'

The officer laughed, 'A bastard to you, but a patriot to me. But he also gives me a problem – I am thinking that if a man changes sides once, maybe he will do it again, eh?' He raised his pistol and shot Ajdin in the forehead.

One of the first lessons you are taught in the security services is that when placed in a situation where the odds are stacked heavily against you, act at the first opportunity. The first opportunity is the first time people's attention is taken off *you*. The officer's action certainly took the soldiers' attention off us as Ajdin slumped to the floor; they were as surprised as we were, but we had the training and seized the opportunity.

I ducked and launched myself into the first soldier bringing up my right arm forcing his rifle to shoot into the ceiling as I punched with all my force into his stomach with my left fist. Gold had taken out the officer by pushing his elbow against the joint so he couldn't aim his pistol and kicking his legs from under him with a sweep of her right leg, sending him to the floor and releasing his grip on the pistol which she took and shot him in the back of the head in one move. I turned my attention to the second soldier, who wasn't sure what to do and was bringing his rifle round to bear on Gold as my straight hand chop hit the back of his neck with such force it broke with an audible crack and both he and his rifle fell to the floor.

We stood and looked at each other.

'Time we were out of here,' I said. We gathered our own guns and I looked carefully outside. At the far side of the compound two security men were hurrying toward us.

'You drive,' said Gold as we ran out to the van. 'Same way out as we came in, there's no other exit.'

I turned the key and thankfully she started first time. We moved off and I turned towards the main house. The security men were now in front of us and although well-armed they waved us through; thankfully they hadn't 'turned'.

****

CHAPTER 15

We left the compound and took the road back into the city; odds were the military would think we had fled the other way, away from the city, and concentrate any search that way. The main city of Antakya is a very built-up modern place – the capital of Hatay province – and very busy on its own accord as well as a busy tourist centre in the season. It was busy with the evening social traffic building up as Gold directed me to a multilevel car park near the centre, I took a ticket from the machine and drove to the top deck.

'Reverse into the parking space,' Gold said.

I was beginning to see her plan.

'You're going to launch the drones from here.'

'Yes.'

'Did Ajdin know the plan? They might be expecting drones.'

'No, he didn't know anything about the drones until we picked them up this morning – and I've been with him since then.'

That was good news. The car park was quite busy with people parking up before going out for a meal or social event. We slipped into the back of the van and squeezed between the two drones and their payloads; the two of us sitting in the front on full view might raise somebody's suspicions, so better off in the back out of sight. The car parks have security patrols and the last thing we wanted was a tap on the window from them. The drones were not military, I'd worked with enough military drones in the past to see that, but they looked substantial; they'd better be to fly with the payload they'd be carrying.

'How are you getting out of here?'I asked.

'Going to book into a cheap hotel for a day and then get a flight back to Cyprus.'

'I've got an SBS boat coming in for me on the shore at one o'clock if you want to join me?'

'No, my Cypriot passport would have been registered when I flew in and if I don't fly back out at some time my cover would be blown. You never know when I might want to come back.'

I don't think I'd ever want to come back, but I could see the sense in what she was saying. Looked like I was going to make the journey to meet Jones alone.

We snoozed and relaxed until the car park had been quiet for a while; one patrol had driven slowly by but the lone occupant seemed more interested in singing along with his radio; loudly and out of tune. It was now just past nine and getting quite dark. Looking from the back through the front windscreen I could see the city lit up like all major cities at night, twinkling lights stretching away into the distance.

Gold checked her watch. 'Right let's get this done then.'

I pushed open the back doors – not totally open as I'd parked about two feet from the car park side wall; any further and I'd be out into the narrow access road between the parking bays and be noticed.

Gold lifted one of the drones to the back of the van by the doors and hooked on a heavy solid steel tube; this, she hoped, would be enough to smash through the warehouse skylight. I just hoped the drone was powerful enough to lift it. It was, and soon Gold had the four blades whirring and the drone lifting from the van out over the car park wall and away. We looked at the controller screen that showed view from the drone camera, the city beneath it.

'Does it know where the warehouse is?' I asked, thinking it might be programmed.

'No, I have to guide it.'

'Do you know where the warehouse is from here?' I asked, knowing full well that Gold doesn't leave things to chance.

She nodded her head. 'Look towards two o'clock about a mile and half away.'

I did so.

'See the red flashing lights?'

I could just about see them through the brown polluted air that hung over the city; they were on top of a tall building that stood out above most of the others around it, I couldn't make out much detail from this distance except the red flashing lights on its roof.

'Yes.'

'That's the warehouse.'

It took a minute or so for the drone to get there and the control screen gave a clear picture of the military compound below that circled round the warehouse. Figures that looked like ants were moving around, and rectangle shapes that I took to be lorries were parked beside it. I watched the screen as Gold moved the drone over the warehouse. The roof was a single slanting one and had three wide skylight windows. She positioned the drone over the middle one about twenty feet above it, which should let gravity accelerate the falling drone and its steel payload enough for it to smash through. We wouldn't know until the second drone was in position whether it had worked, as Gold had to cut the power to let the first drone fall and hit the skylight.

'Fingers crossed,' she said and cut the radio signal to the drone.

As she did so the control screen blanked out. Quickly I passed the second controller to her and moved the second drone to the rear doors. Then I carefully moved the shoe box-sized incendiary and explosive bomb and waited until Gold had switched on the controller and taken the drone up to about two feet above the car park wall before jumping out and hooking on the box and very carefully pressing in a button that primed the explosive charge to explode on impact. And then it was flying away as I got back into the van and pulled the rear doors closed. We watched the controller screen and saw the city pass beneath the drone camera until it reached the military compound. By now the smashing of the window and the drone falling inside the warehouse must have caused a bit of panic. It had. We could see soldiers running around; most seemed to be running away from the warehouse.

'It must have got through and fallen on the warehouse floor – they think the steel tube is a bomb, which is why they are running away,' explained Gold, even though I hadn't asked the question.

The second drone was spotted, and several flashes from rifles being shot could be seen, but she moved it out of sight over the warehouse before any AK-47s or similar carbine could pump lead into the sky. I watched the controller screen as Gold moved it over the smashed window and lowered it slowly down and through into the warehouse. The camera showed the warehouse lights on and stacks of wooden crates of all sizes in rows; crates similar to those in the Purley warehouse. Part of the floor was covered in upright standing warheads and shells of all sizes.

I was taken aback. 'My God, you could equip an army with that lot.'

'Yes, but which army – Assad's, the Houthis, ISIS, al-Qaeda? I don't think we want that lot getting in any of their hands.' She exaggeratedly raised a finger and switched off the drone's power.

We looked expectantly through the night towards the red flashing lights on the warehouse roof. Nothing happened. Had the explosive failed? Then the red lights went out, and we waited with baited breath; surely we'd see some flames?

The one flame we did see was massive, absolutely massive! It took the roof with it way up into the night sky and behind it flame continued to pour out of the warehouse upwards, accelerated by explosions we could plainly hear from our position a mile and a half away. We must have hit a dynamite stockpile, and a big one at that.

I don't know why, but we both started to laugh – relief of the tension? We gave a high five. Sirens were beginning to be heard, growing in number, and blue flashing lights lit up the sky from the streets.

'Time to go,' I said. I had a long journey back to the rendezvous point and wanted plenty of time, as I didn't fancy missing the one o'clock deadline and hanging around that beach for twenty-four hours until the next one.

'Okay.' Gold took out a tunic from the rucksack and put it on over her onesie before wrapping the hijab around her head. She clasped her hands together and gave me a slight bow.

'See you in Cyprus. Take care.' And with that she turned and made her way to the car park staircase.

****

CHAPTER 16

I gave her five minutes, sitting and watching the inferno in the distance and hearing muffled explosions before driving out of the car park and turning towards the Syrian border road, the one we had come in on. I kept checking my mirror but I suppose every patrol had been called to the compound. Except one, and that one had set up a roadblock half a mile in front of me, probably because of the happenings with Ajdin and the soldiers at the big house; it was too soon for the warehouse attack to have gotten through to those in charge and roadblocks to have been ordered.

It was only one patrol, three soldiers and a jeep; the jeep was parked sideways on but wasn't long enough to block the whole road. I thought about winging it, hitting its front corner and disabling a wheel so they couldn't chase me, but that could disable the van as well - no, best to take advantage of the element of surprise and put some distance between them and me. I opened the driver's side window and pulled out my Sig. Flicking the headlights full on I floored the accelerator; they wouldn't realise the speed I was doing until I was nearly on them. Surprise is a great element in warfare, and even in a small scenario like this one it works. At about fifty yards from them the soldiers started to think that maybe I wasn't going to stop, but before they could unsling their rifles I was firing the Sig from outside the side window which had them running for cover, and then I was past and well away into the darkness, lights out, before they started to fire after me.

I kept my foot hard to the floor. I could see the ocean a half mile on my right shimmering in the moonlight beyond the woods. It wouldn't be long before the jeep would catch me up, so time to play games. I pulled up on the right-hand side of the road and moved into the bushes on the left side. I found a fallen tree and lay behind it, my CF8 aimed at the road. Right on cue, the jeep arrived. They stopped fifty yards down the road as soon as they saw the van and two of the three soldiers got out and walked, half hidden behind it with their rifles up as it moved slowly forward – at least they had some training! I'd left the van driver's door open to look like I'd made a quick escape; they approached it slowly and after some chat spread out twenty feet apart and started to enter the undergrowth towards the sea. I gave them five minutes and then crept over the road, and keeping to the side of the jeep they wouldn't be able to see I took my knife and punctured the two tyres; then I was back into the van and away.

I took out my mobile, turned it on and brought up the location app; the red dot where I had set it on the beach was flashing, but it was still quite a way to go and reinforcements for the soldiers would be on their way as soon as they got back to the jeep and radioed in. At least the moonlight gave me the option of driving without lights which would keep my position a bit more secure. I checked the time – shit! Quarter to one and I still had to cross half a mile of thick undergrowth on foot to get to the shore after reaching the right place on the road. The bloody accelerator wouldn't go down any further. I hoped Jones would be a bit lax with his clock; stupid thing was I should have put the comms in my rucksack and then I'd be able to contact him, I but I hadn't as any transmission between us could easily be picked up and give the location away.

I pulled up at the roadside a hundred metres before I got parallel with the beach where the app was flashing. I couldn't hide the van so I drove it as far as I could into the scrub on the other side of the road; that might give me a bit more time and confuse whoever was going to come after me that I'd gone inland. I ran the final hundred metres and turned into the sloping scrub and forest, trying hard to pick my feet up and take long steps rather than push through and leave an obvious trail. Mind you, if my chasers had dogs then I'd better get into the water as soon as I could.

I made it the beach without hearing or seeing any activity up on the road. I went to the water's edge and strained my eyes looking for a boat shape in the dark waves offshore; nothing, but at least there wasn't a storm to contend with. Taking out my torch I started with the three short and one long signal Jones had said to use. Checking the time on my mobile it was one ten – had they been and gone? I carried on flashing, forming a plan in my mind of what to do if I got no response. No doubt the Turkish Military would launch a full scale search for me at daybreak, so the best plan would be for me go back to the road and away the other side of it, or maybe take the van and drive further along the road towards the Syrian border and hide up there. I wouldn't think the Turks wanted to do anything military near that border which could be used as provocation by the Syrians and their Russian masters.

I thought I saw a light between the waves. I did, I saw it again. I kept flashing my signal and soon the dark outline of the FB was visible between the waves coming towards me. My elation was killed as the sounds of sirens and motor engines filtered down from the road, I looked back and it seemed the whole of the road was filling up with headlights and vehicles pulling up. Voices echoed through the trees – Christ! It seemed the whole Turkish army were coming for me. I waded out as fast as I could to meet the FB, which was making its way towards me bouncing through the waves.

'You just about made it then,' said Jones, pulling me aboard. 'Another couple of minutes and we would have gone. What the hell's going on up there at the road – are they after you?

I fell into the boat with a feeling of great relief as Taylor increased the revs a little, not enough to be heard on land, and we headed out to sea.

'Yes, I blew up their ammo dump. I don't think they liked that.'

The whistle of bullets through the air above us had Jones flinging himself down joining me on the boat floor with Williams. Williams looked at Jones.

'Return fire, sir? We have company starboard side?'

We looked, and there about a mile away the lights of three fast Turkish Naval skiffs were heading our way lights blazing in the darkness.

'Bloody Hell! Get onto base and have some support come out to meet us. Taylor, open her up.'

The FB jolted into warp speed as Taylor pushed the engines to max and hit the injector switch. Williams got on the radio and Jones pulled open a compartment door on the boat floor and lifted out a bazooka and pointed to a box of rockets inside. 'You know how to load one of these, Nevis?'

'Yes.'

'Okay, grab those and let's go.' He hoisted the tube onto his shoulder, positioning the shoulder stop flange and knelt on the starboard side, aiming it over the edge of the FB. Took a rocket from the box and opened the bazooka lid – that's the end cover – pushed in a rocket until it clicked into the breach before closing it and securing the hasp. I tapped Jones hard on the shoulder. 'Ready,' I shouted and ducked away covering my ears.

The third one we fired hit home and the nearest skiff which was still a good six hundred metres from us went up in an explosion of fire as the rocket exploded on impact leaving burning pieces of the boat floating on the sea.

We were now pretty much out of range of anything shot from the shore and the FB's twin Mercedes engines were showing their class, putting evermore distance between us and the chasing skiffs.

'What the...?' Williams pointed towards the skiffs. Behind them and catching up fast were two Turkish Naval launches with machine guns mounted on the forward superstructure. We were out of range, but those boats can move so we wouldn't be for much longer. I tapped Jones on the shoulder and shouted in his ear what we had seen. He moved his head from the bazooka sights and looked.

'Jesus, Nevis! Are you sure you blew up an ammo dump and not the President's palace?' He shouted over his shoulder to Taylor. 'Weave!'

Taylor started to zigzag weave the boat. Then we heard the sound that strikes fear into any soldier out in the open: the whirring of helicopter blades.

It was a good way away from us and coming from the direction of the beach.

'Are we in international waters?' Jones shouted to Taylor, who nodded 'Affirmative.'

I knew what Jones was thinking. We wouldn't stand a chance against a 'copter out here in the open waters, especially if it was carrying air to ground missiles, so we would raise the white flag and surrender. Doing that in international waters would limit the chances of being held for more than a couple of days; our masters would say we were just on patrol and must have strayed out of the Cypriot three-mile limit. But if we were in Turkish waters that was a different thing all together; we'd be put on a show trial no doubt, and either rot in a Tukish jail or be part of a prisoner swap.

The whoosh of a missile had us all diving to the bottom of the boat – seems they didn't want to take prisoners. I was wrong; the distant boom of it hitting home on one of the Turkish launches that disintegrated in a white explosion of flame and debris shooting into the air stopped my thoughts for a moment. Then as one we all turned and looked towards the Cyprus coast. Bearing down on us were two SBS Pacific 24 Mark 4 Royal Navy armed launches – the missile had come from one of them; the firepower they had far outclassed the Turkish launches. Our chasers had seen them too, the other launch and skiffs turned for home and the helicopter banked away towards the land.

In a minute the first Pacific drew close by and a smiling face looked down on us from the rail.

'I might have known it would be you upsetting the neighbours Jonesy, any casualties?'

Jones saluted. 'No sir, glad to see you, sir.'

He was bloody right there.

****

CHAPTER 17

Back at the base on Cyprus we learnt that the Pacifics had been on patrol in international waters looking for people traffickers' boats coming from Syria when they picked up Williams's call for assistance.

And that was it – no debriefing, no written statements to do and sign, nothing. Woodward had said I didn't exist, that I wasn't there and the powers that be would deny all knowledge of me, but that was par for the course in my N14 days, so no change there.

After a hot shower and a good sleep I wandered down to the restaurant and joined Jones and his crew for a full English breakfast – not as tasty as a Turkish one, but after a day without food it did the job.

'I don't know what you were doing in Turkey, Nevis, but you opened up a can of worms.' Jones spoke between mouthfuls of sausage and fried potato. 'Whatever you blew up could be seen from the spy satellites – the base is on red alert. You certainly annoyed somebody.'

'Couldn't be me – I'm not even here.'

They all laughed.

I was surprised Woodward didn't ring to congratulate me, but I suppose it was to be expected as the Turks would have increased radio and telephone traffic surveillance in the hope of picking up some evidence of who the bomber was. I gave Gold a call.

'You still there?'

'Yes, some cheap hotel with musty bed sheets – lovely.'

'What about Rambart, any sign of her?'

'I'll ring you on a burner.'

'Okay.' I closed my phone; she'd ring me back on a disposable burner phone and then ditch it after the call – anybody picking up the call wouldn't have a chance of tracing it. Can't be too careful. My phone rang and she was back.

'The whole place is at fever pitch – we must have knocked out most of their stored armaments. There's a cafe opposite the Defence Ministry here and I've basically taken up residence. Rambart's been in and out of there with some high ranking officers. They're turning over the old town – the rumour on the street and in the daily papers is that it was the Kurds, the PKK.'

'Right,' that made sense – Turkey's main enemy is the Kurdistan Worker's Party, or PKK; they claim to represent Turkey's largest ethnic group, the Kurds, who make up twenty percent of the Turkish population. They've been battling the Turkish state off and on for some thirty years demanding independence, and if the Turks can blame the PKK for anything they will as it gives them an excuse to crack down on them with superior firepower. Mind you, that firepower would have been a bit diminished now.

‘How long are you staying?’ I asked Gold.

‘A couple more days – the security at the airport has been ramped up, so I’ll let that cool down a bit and fly back to Cyprus and then London. What about you?’

‘I think I’m out of here later on a freight flight to Stansted.’

‘Okay, take care.’

‘You too.’

Click.

****

I was indeed put on the freight flight to Stansted and expected Woodward to meet me as I came down the gangway – nobody, not even a car to get me home. I felt like sending him a rude text but decided to stay professional. *Yes, I know, makes a change!* Woodward obviously had no intention of being seen with me, just in case anybody had put two and two together and linked me being out of the country and returning on a freight flight from Cyprus with the Turkish explosion. What if one of the civilians working the Cyprus base was feeding information to the Turks? It's quite possible, if not very probable. Word of my appearance at the base, my disappearance at the time of the warehouse attack, my reappearance afterwards and the deploying of the SBS could be put together to give a possible scenario and get the British Ambassador called into the Turkish Defence ministry and shouted at. No proof though, but a photo of Clarence Woodward, Head of MI6, greeting me at Stansted would complete the jigsaw. If you check the perimeters of any military airfield you'll find a band of weather hardy plane fanatics with their ears tuned to the control tower and their cameras clicking away at the planes and personnel. You've probably guessed what I'm going to tell you next – yes, not all these nerds are real nerds; in amongst them will be a few foreign embassy employees, clicking away with their Diplomatic Immunity papers in their pocket. Information is the most valuable commodity in the international spying game.

It was nice to sleep in my own bed and well past nine before I rose the next morning. I sat with a cup of coffee, looking through the

French doors that led out to my balcony at the Thames and the river traffic as I thought through my position. The basic job of killing one or both of the Rambarts had been compromised by Woodward's intervention. His request, or should I say order, had been carried out; he now knew both Rambarts were arms-dealing to the Turks and any missile sales from them to a terrorist organisation had been knocked on the head – that is until they sent another lot through. Perhaps I should have a quiet word with him – MI6 isn't adverse to knocking off somebody who poses a threat to the UK. If I could get a verbal contract, and it would only ever be a verbal one, with a few grand attached, then this whole thing could end up as quite a good earner for Gold and me.

I wandered into the office at about 10.30 and half an hour later Woodward and his goons arrived; I was expecting them – he would have had my apartment and office under surveillance since I got back.

He fluttered his handkerchief over the chair seat before sitting down. I suppose if you go around in a beige Crombie you have to be a bit careful; I made a mental note to put a bit of chewing gum on the seat edge prior to his next visit.

'Well Nevis, glad you got out in one piece,' he said, pushing the handkerchief into a side pocket. 'You seem to have gone a bit over the top – our Ambassador has been called in at Ankara and I myself have had to endure a rather brusque meeting with the Minister of Defence, and all our Mediterranean bases are now on red alert. Your action reminds me somewhat of a line in my favourite film: '*You were only supposed to blow the bloody doors off.*'

Thankfully he didn't try to copy Michael Caine's Cockney accent.

'You did tell me to destroy the missiles,' I reminded him.

'Indeed I did, Nevis, and you successfully achieved that with a little help from the SBS by sinking the freighter. Mission accomplished – home, James.'

'His name's Jones.'

'What?'

'The SBS commander who was with me – Jones, not James.'

'It's an idiom.' He paused and took a deep breath, doubting my knowledge of the word's meaning, 'Google it.'

'So if my mission is accomplished like you say, that's it, I'm out?'

'Well I really don't think I can let you do anymore damage, do you? Two dead at

Purley and God knows how many on the freighter and in Antakya. You're a walking Grim Reaper.'

'What about the Rambarts?'

'My department will cover that – you just carry on with handling security for Eve Rambart as she asked you, and feed me back any relevant information on her and her husband's arms dealing.'

I'd forgotten about that little lie I'd told Woodward about being hired for security reasons. I nodded. 'Okay.'

'Has she been in contact since she's been back?'

My heart skipped a beat – *since she'd been back?* Gold would have surely let me know if Eve Rambart was on her way back to the UK. Now all of a sudden I was worried about Gold; was she all right? Had her cover been broken?

'I didn't know she was back,' I said as calmly as I could.

Woodward nodded, 'Must have flown in last night – she's been seen at the apartment. I take it she didn't see you at anytime in Turkey?'

'No.'

'Good. I wouldn't like to be in your shoes if she had recognised you.'

'Why don't you arrest her? You've got the photos of her getting on the ship.'

'Not enough – she could have just been a passenger to Turkey taking a holiday. Freighters do carry the odd passenger.'

'Naval freighters?'

'I want to let her run, Nevis – see who else we might net in the Rambarts' circle of business partners. So it could be useful having you on the inside with Eve Rambart. But just remember that as far as my department goes, you don't exist.' He stood and brushed down the back of his coat. 'Good day, Nevis.' He stopped at the door and turned back. 'Oh, and as far as I personally am concerned, well done.' He gave me the briefest of smiles and was gone.

The first thing I thought was that Woodward hadn't taken back his mobile; people like him don't forget things like that, crafty bugger.

The second thing I thought was, how the hell did Eve Rambart get back to the UK without Gold knowing? I took a burner from the drawer and dialled her number.

'Yeah?'

'You okay?'

'Wonderful, my clothes are beginning to smell as musty as the bed. Hang on, I'll go outside – too many people in this café. Everybody's on edge; there's a fifty thousand lira reward for information leading to an arrest.'

I could hear a babble of talking and chairs scraping on a tiled floor as she left the cafe.

'Okay, all clear now.'

'Why didn't you tell me Rambart had flown out?'

There was a brief silence. 'She hasn't, she's still here.'

'Woodward says she flew into London last night.'

'He's wrong – I've seen her go into the Defence Ministry again and she hasn't come out yet.'

'So who did his men see in her apartment last night?' I was asking myself the question as well.

'It wasn't Eve Rambart.'

'Something funny going on here.'

'Perhaps she's sent a double to take the heat away from here? She must realise she's in the frame for illegal arms-dealing after the freighter and warehouse explosions; pretty obvious to her that somebody's trying to disrupt the business. She's definitely still here.'

'Okay, I think I'll go and get a visual at her apartment – see who it is.' I could hear sirens in the background over the phone.

'I've got company, I'm fifty metres from the cafe and a jeep full of armed police has just stormed in. I'm off – I'll give the hotel a miss, I've got my passport and cards with me so I'll go to the airport and see if I can get a flight out; if not I'll mingle with the departure crowds – it's a busy airport so I should be able to blend in.'

'Okay.'

'I'll call you, don't call me.'

Click.

****

CHAPTER 18

Knightsbridge was busy – isn't it always? The jostling crowds of shoppers made it impossible to see if I had a tail. Gold would have spotted one in an instant. I was taking a chance but I needed to know if in fact Eve Rambart was back home or somebody else was being used to create a diversion for her.

The street door into the office block we watched from was open; it was only 3-o'clock, business hours, I made my way up the stairs to the first floor and checked the office we'd been in before; it was still empty so I used my debit card to slip open the Yale lock on the door and went inside. I left the door ajar so anybody seeing it would think I was a prospective tenant taking a look; the landlord wouldn't be around – these places are owned by major investment companies and they do everything through agents.

I looked across the road to Eve Rambart's apartment and took a small pair of binoculars from my pocket and homed in on the windows. The blinds were open and I could see through the lounge into the kitchen where she was sitting at the breakfast bar, drinking a cup of something and reading a magazine. Woodward was right, she was home – Gold had missed her somehow.

I could do the job right now: walk across the road, up the stairs, ring the bell and bang bang – be a million pounds richer when Nicholas Rambart paid me out. If he paid me out, I certainly wouldn't be meeting him to collect the promised fee – probably collect a bullet not a cheque if I did. No, he could do a bank transfer and then I'd make good my debt to Eve Rambart, you see I have got some principles, kill him and be safe. But I wasn't going to do the job right now; as I said before, I plan jobs, plan them to the slightest detail. I knew where the bodies would end up: a council crematorium in Streatham. I had a cash deal with two of the workers. Money talks, even in death.

My phone rang. It was Gold.

'I'm on a local flight back to Cyprus.'

'Well done, you got out alright then?'

'Yes, so much confusion at the airport it was quite easy.'

'Good, I'm in that Knightsbridge office overlooking Rambart's place – she's inside, Woodward was right.'

'He wasn't.'

'What do you mean, *he wasn't*?'

'Eve Rambart is on this flight sitting four rows in front of me.'

I was silent for a moment checking the binoculars. There she was, sitting at the breakfast bar. 'Are you sure?'

'Totally.'

'Then who am I looking at in the apartment?'

'Or who am I looking at sitting four rows in front of me on the plane?

'Two Eve Rambarts?'

We both said the obvious in unison. 'Twins?'

My mind raced. 'That's brilliant, bloody brilliant. One acts normally and is on show, whilst the other's hidden in the background doing the dirty deals. Jesus, it's brilliant!'

'What do you want me to do, stay with her? What if she gets a flight from Lanarka to Heathrow?'

'Let me know. I think she probably will – nothing in Cyprus to interest her. Just let me know and I'll pick her up at Heathrow and see where she goes, and then you get a later flight back here.'

'Okay. Do you think Nicholas Rambart knows about the twin?'

'I don't know, I really don't – I don't even know if they are working together. He was in the Purley warehouse with the missiles and she was on the boat with them to Turkey, and yet they want each other killed. Something's not right. Get back and we'll dig a bit more.'

'Okay.'

I closed my phone. What the hell was going on? There was only one way to find out.

I weaved my way through the slow traffic across the road to the leather shop, looking out for anybody that might be one of Woodward's people; nobody stood out, but surveillance operatives are bloody good at their job so you can't be sure. I knew what I was going to do next – an old ploy that I'd used before to clear a building. The door to Rambart's apartment block was open, so I went in and stood quietly in the ground floor hallway and listened for any movement on the upper landings. All was quiet. I soon changed that with one hit at the fire alarm glass with my elbow. The siren wailed out as I left the building and waited at the leather shop doorway.

'What's going on?' asked the sales assistant as two of them came out.

'Fire alarm I think,' I shrugged. 'Can't see any smoke though.'

A small crowd was gathering fast and residents were coming out of the building looking worried and asking each other what was happening, some clutching bags of treasured possessions.

And there she was: Eve Rambart came down the entrance steps and joined the increasing throng. Only she wasn't Eve Rambart; she looked enough like Rambart to be mistaken from a short distance away, but she wasn't Eve Rambart – or was she? I edged into the crowd and got nearer to her; I wanted to make sure my eyes weren't playing tricks. I moved to her left and got the view I wanted. There was no big diamond wedding ring on the finger on the left hand – this wasn't Eve Rambart. So who are you then lady, and what game are you playing?

The fire brigade arrived and caused traffic chaos parking in the road – must have been a quiet day for them, three tenders and a car? Pretty soon they had checked out the building and a rumour had spread through the crowd that it must have been '*bloody kids smashing the alarm again.*'

****

CHAPTER 19

Nothing I could do now, except wait for the real Eve Rambart to get back and see what happens. Gold checked back later and said Rambart had bought a ticket for a Heathrow flight the next morning and booked into a hotel near the airport; she would wait for a later one so Rambart didn't clock her on both flights, and she would also book a different hotel. I decided not to go to Heathrow and follow Eve Rambart from there; I was far more interested in the lady in the apartment. Who was she, and why was she there?

I went back to my office; if Nicholas Rambart suspected me of being involved in the warehouse raid at Purley he would surely have come after me by now? No reason why he should think I was involved, but with people like him suspicion is the best defence.

I checked the times of the flights from Cyprus the next day; first one got in about 11.30am, so give Eve Rambart an hour to go through customs and get to Knightsbridge, which means she should be there about 12.30.

****

I had a slow breakfast, checked the flight was on time – it was – and made my way back to the empty Knightsbridge office.

There was some movement and voices from the same floor as I started up the stairs; I stopped and prayed in my mind that the landlord hadn't let the place. A door shut and the voices stopped – must have been another office. I carried on and settled on an old chair to wait for Eve Rambart to arrive opposite.

The doppelganger was there. I watched through my binoculars; she seemed to be tidying the place up – no, hang on, she was *packing* the place up. Drawers were being emptied into archive-size boxes and clothes being brought through from the bedroom and stacked on the sofa and chairs. Whoever this lady was she was getting ready to move out.

Eve Rambart got out of a taxi outside the leather shop at 12.45 and made her way into the building. Through the windows I could see the look-a-like was having a drink at the breakfast bar; she rose and went into the bedroom, half closing the door behind her. A few moments later Eve Rambart came into view; she stood still, looking around, too far away for me to see her expression, but the body language said she wasn't expecting the apartment to be packed up and ready to go. The bedroom door opened and the look-a-like came in, raised her hand and shot Eve Rambart, who crumpled to the floor out of my sight. Look-a-like stepped over and shot again at where the hidden body would be. This lady, whoever she was, was a pro, this was planned; one to the body to bring the target down, and probably one to the head to finish the job.

I was stunned, my mind was blank. If I didn't know what was going on before, my head was now in a brain maze; nothing was making sense.

The look-a-like made a mobile call and within minutes a large removal van had pulled up outside, half on, half off the pavement, and four men in overalls were on their way up to the apartment; a fifth stayed with the van, opened the rear doors and let the ramp down. This was professional, very professional.

It took twenty minutes at the outside before everything that was to be removed from the apartment had been put in the lorry, it was everything except the furniture. Maybe the rental agreement was for 'furnished accommodation', so that had to stay – everything else, all reference to the person who had rented it, which I presume was Eve Rambart, was gone. The last thing out was Eve herself – or I presume it was, inside a large rolled rug tied at both end and carried out by three of the men. A professional job, very professional. I made my way down to the street; the lorry had no markings on the side or back, and I took the number as it drove off – it would be false. I could follow in a cab but any pro would soon suss that. That's why Ubers are so useful – ordinary cars don't stand out like cabs; but by the time I ordered one and it got to me through the London traffic, the lorry would be well gone.

I rang Clancy at the Yard. Dick Clancy and I had worked together on many cases when I with the OC Unit at the Yard; he was pretty high up now and would have unfettered access to surveillance programmes.

'Nevis, long time no contact. I thought you'd retired to the coast like you always said you would?'

'Nah, not yet, Dick – not old enough for that yet. I thought you'd be an AC by now, office on the fifth floor and spend the day pushing paper clips around the desk, and choosing between a custard cream or a digestive with you coffee.'

He laughed. 'Bollocks, when they offer me that I'll be round to you for a job. Anyway, what do you want?'

'Got a pen?'

'Yes.'

'See if you can do an ANPR on a vehicle for me, just today's journey.' I gave him the lorry number.

'Person of interest?' he asked.

'Most definitely. It's on a lorry but probably false plates.'

That was the great benefit of ANPR, it traced the plate whatever it was on.

'When do you want the info?' asked Clancy.

'Tomorrow morning will do fine.'

'Okay, I'll give you a bell.'

'Thanks Dick, I owe you.'

'Yeah, you say that every time. I reckon my credit with you must be pretty high by now. Talk tomorrow.'

And he rang off.

The lorry's route and where it took the deceased Eve Rambart would hopefully provide a few answers as to what and who I was dealing with. Whoever it was had just cost me one million pounds, or eight hundred thousand pounds, or both. I couldn't claim the eight hundred thousand from Eve if I killed Nicholas, and I couldn't claim the million from Nicholas for killing Eve.

****

Clancy woke me at seven the next morning. He always was the first in the office and the last to leave; it's a habit you can fall into if you've no family – work becomes your family. He told me what I thought he would: the lorry ended up at a warehouse on an industrial estate in Purley. I took the postcode from Clancy to check it, just to make sure Nicholas Rambart hadn't got two warehouses in Purley; he hadn't, the code checked to the one I'd been in.

Gold arrived back early afternoon and travelled into London on the Piccadilly Line, changing onto the Bakerloo Line at Piccadilly Circus for Charing Cross and met me in our usual station cafe. I brought her up to speed.

'We need to know who that lady in Rambart's apartment is – she's the key to all this. If she can handle a hit then she's a pro,' Gold said.

'Yes, but working for who?'

'Got to be Nicholas if the body ended up at Purley, must be. This coffee is crap compared to the stuff in Turkey,' she said, putting her cup down and pulling a face. Subtlety isn't in Gold's dictionary.

'So Nicholas kills his own wife?'

'He offered you a million to do it, perhaps he couldn't wait any longer?'

'Why bother with a look-a-like? Just do the job and that's that?'

'He obviously needs to create the impression Eve's still around maybe?'

'I think I need to try and get a meet with Nicholas.'

'Dangerous.' She pushed the coffee cup aside. 'Not as dangerous as British Rail coffee, but dangerous.'

****

I tried contacting Rambart at the Hilton, pretending to be a financial journalist wanting to do a piece on his success. It was always an answer phone and my recorded messages were never replied to. I tried for two days and then decided to go full frontal.

'I nearly didn't recognise you, you look quite the rich boy about town,' Gold laughed. She was in the Podium Bar at the Hilton as I came and sat opposite her on the third day at lunch time. If I was going to wander around the Hilton's corridors I had to look the part: the dark blue Savile Row suit and matching shirt and tie hadn't been out of the wardrobe since a protection job for an opera diva who was being bombarded with death threats a couple of years ago; you can't work in the Opera Houses of Europe in faded jeans, a Status Quo T-shirt and Skechers.

I laughed. ‘You think I fit in then?’

‘Oh yes, eyes turned when you came in the Bar – especially the female ones.’

‘Well that’s no good then – I’m supposed to fit in, not stand out.’

‘You’ll do. What’s the plan?’

‘The plan is to get into Nicholas Rambart’s suite and bug it.’

‘How?’

‘No idea, but I noticed at the reception desk his room number key card is in the pigeonhole, so it’s empty at the moment.’

Gold’s mind flicked into operational mode; I knew she would be able to find a way in. She stood and buttoned her coat. ‘I’ll see you on the third floor.’

****

CHAPTER 20

Major hotels are always busy – always people arriving and leaving, always a queue at reception, always a lack of porters – and with over four hundred and fifty rooms the Hilton foyer is always a mini traffic jam.

Gold gave a cursory glance at the pigeon holes behind the reception desk – 324's keycard was still there. She walked around the outside of the crowd to the main doors and stood to one side of them, pretending to look at the display of tourist *places to visit* leaflets; she knew what she was looking for and it wasn't a tourist leaflet, it was a tourist. She and waited and watched. Pretty soon the mark arrived: a family in a taxi overloaded with cases who declined the offer of help from the doorman to call a porter to carry anything. Gold waited until the family had dumped their first cases inside the doors and had gone out for more. She moved through the jostling crowd, seized the biggest, heaviest looking case and struggled with it away through the crush to the side. She tapped a doorman on the arm.

'Could I have some help with this please? I'm just getting over a knee replacement and have to be a bit careful. It's not very heavy.'

The doorman leapt into action, chastising himself for not noticing this young lady struggling with her case and beckoned a porter over. 'Take this for the lady.'

The porter picked up the case. 'Room number, madam?'

'324, third floor suite.' Gold made a limping move towards the desk. 'I'll get my key.'

The doorman halted her.

'You go to the lift, madam – I'll get your key or you'll be queuing for ages.' And he did just that, dodging through the crowd to the head of the reception queue, asking for and getting suite 324's key card and hurrying back to the lift where Gold and the porter were waiting.

'There we are, madam. Is there anything else I can help you with?'

'No, no, thank you so much.' Gold smiled as she pressed a five pound note into his hand and took the keycard, 'Thank you so much, so helpful.'

The lift doors closed and it ascended, disgorging residents on the first and second floors and Gold and the porter on the third. The porter walked along to 324 and waited at the door as Gold 'limped' to join him.

'I can manage from here.' Another five pound note was gratefully received. 'Thank you so much.'

The porter bowed. 'You're welcome, madam.' Then he made his way to the staff stairs at the end of the corridor, pocketing the fiver.

I arrived, having watched Gold's subterfuge and then taken the public stairs. Gold had the door open and I lifted in the suitcase and joined her inside, closing the door behind me. It was a luxurious suite; the furniture was modern and looked brand new, a ninety-inch plasma TV screen was on the wall, fresh flowers in an array of vases on all the side tables, and a quick scout round showed housekeeping had replenished the bathroom toiletries and bed coverings. No kitchen, all food was ordered from a menu on the main table and delivered from the hotel's kitchens. I could settle into this life quite nicely.

Gold broke into my dreams of luxurious living. 'I'm going down to keep a watch on the reception desk. I'll give them back the key card so as not to cause a panic if Rambart comes asking for it. If they do, I'll text your mobile.'

'Right.'

She left and I slipped the security chain on the door, just in case. I took out my mobile and put it on the table; I didn't want to miss the text if it came – Nicholas Rambart wouldn't take too kindly to finding me in his suite. I slipped on a pair of thin latex gloves and began looking.

I started at the desk, pulling out the papers from its drawers one by one and skipping through them, looking for anything that might refer to arms. The third drawer down was the one: business papers filed in coloured manila envelopes similar to the ones I'd found at the Purley warehouse. They held invoices for millions of pounds from various arms producers in the UK, for weapons from pistols to missiles; a blue envelope had financial information photocopied from various money and financial journals and newspapers about companies that I recognised as other ordnance manufacturers, with notes scribbled on them in various places. The contents of a red envelope set me back on my heels: it was obituary notices cut from newspapers. I knew a couple of the names and pictures, they were CEOs of multinational conglomerates when they were alive – why would Rambart have those in a file?

I took pictures of them, four in all, and then a few of the invoices. The last file was plain but the content wasn't: a black-and-white photo of our look-a-like lady was stapled to a copy of a sheet of typed paper; it was in a foreign language but the large heading and official hand stamp made it quite obvious where it was from: Turkey.

My phone buzzed. I looked at the text from Gold: *'Look-a-like coming up.'*

I took a photo of the page and taking a last look around the room to make sure everything was where it was when I came in I hurried out, closed the door behind me and took the stairs down.

'Anything?' Gold was a lady of few words.

'Yes, I think so. Do you like doner kebab?'

Gold gave me a quizzical look but didn't ask me to clarify my seemingly irrelevant question.

'I've got a load of pics of company papers and what look like invoices, plus some peculiar obituaries and what I hope is an answer to who our look-a-like lady is. Where's your car?'

'Up the road in the underground car park.'

We made our way out of the crowded foyer, Gold remembering to limp a little in case the doorman was around and recognised her, and then across the pedestrian crossing to the Hyde

Park side of Park Lane and along to the car park. Parking your motor nearby or inside the car park of the place you are targeting is a basic no-no, as the Hatton Garden safe deposit thieves found out to their cost with Kenny's white Mercedes!

We pulled out onto Park Lane.

'Where to?'

'The office, I want to scan these pics and print them off.'

****

At the Borough she parked in her space in the basement and we went up to the office. I switched on the printer; it's one of those that scans, prints, copies, does the washing up, hoovers the flat and orders a take away – I wish.

I plugged my phone in and scanned the photos picking out the ones from the Hilton to print. I did the Turkish paper one first, enlarging it to A4 size which made it easy to read. I took it out of the tray as the other page photos started to come through.

Gold picked up the others and laid them out on the desk.

'Interesting,' she said.

'What is?' I asked.

She waved a hand to silence me and opened up my desk laptop. 'There's a pattern –

give me some time, I'm going to dig around. Don't interrupt. Pen.'

I gave her a pen and writing pad from the desk drawer and sat opposite. I'd seen her do this before; her cyber experience in Mossad had given her a pretty good idea of where on the net and dark web to go to get answers. Her fingers flashed over the keyboard and every now and then she made notes. I craned forward to read them.

'Go away, you're putting me off.'

I retreated to the kitchen and made two cups of coffee –French type, not even a nod of thanks when I put hers on the desk. I took mine and stood by the window, watching the people and traffic in the high street below. Everybody down there had a home, a life, a story, maybe a family; most would have problems too, money, marriage, job, health. And there we all were, thrown together by this thing called fate to be in the same place on the same planet at the same time; and we'd never know each other than by a passing glimpse maybe. I bet there's some great stories walking along Borough High Street.

Ten minutes of that was enough – my imagination was getting the better of me. I went back to my chair, unnoticed by Gold. I should have taken an *Evening Standard* paper off the free stand at the front of the building. Not only was I bored, I was getting hungry too.

'Back in ten minutes – don't answer the phone,' I instructed Gold. She nodded without giving me a glance, not that she would answer the phone. I picked up the printed page with the Turkish identity at the top and left.

A hundred metres down the Borough High Street from the office I pushed open the door to the Kurzine restaurant; it was still early for diners so Mehmet, the owner was arranging his wine bottles behind the bar. His kebab bars turned slowly, taking the heat from their upright grilles and dripping fat into the trays beneath. He smiled when he saw me.

'Mr Nevis, how are you sir? You haven't been here lately.'

'Hello Mehmet.' We shook hands. 'I've been away. I want two tasty doner kebabs with salad and some advice.'

Mehmet said something in Turkish to one of the staff who attended to the kebabs, putting two flatbreads into the toaster and slicing down the shards of meat into a tray.

Mehmet turned back to me. 'Advice? What advice can I give you? You want to know how to make a kebab?' He laughed.

I gave him the Turkish page. 'Tell me what this is all about.'

He read the page, every now and again he raised his eyes and looked at me with a worried expression. When he finished reading it he slowly put the paper down on the counter and looked at me. He spoke slowly, 'This is official Turkish Government business, not for you. This is trouble.'

'Trouble?'

'This lady they talk about, she is government employee – government defence ministry employee, she is a very high up person in army. Where you get this, Mr Nevis? This it says top secret at top.' He pointed to some words. 'This about missiles and working with Republic Guard in Iran – this is dangerous. Burn it, Mr Nevis – burn it.'

'What's her name?'

He looked down to the paper. 'Aydin, Serife Aydin.'

'You are a star Mehmet, thank you.' I took back the paper.

The chap at the kebab counter called over, asking if I wanted sauce – of course I did, you can't have a kebab without the traditional sauce.

I paid Mehmet, who was still looking at me through worried eyes as he made a great pretence of not accepting my money, but he always does that and he always takes it in the end.

'No no no, you get free, Mr Nevis,' he said, raising his palms towards me. It's been like that since the day four years ago when I went in for a takeaway and found panic in the place. Mehmet's fourteen year-old daughter had disappeared at the same time as one of his young counter assistants; he'd tried to stamp out the relationship and sacked the boy, but as usual with kids that had made it worse and now his daughter had stormed out. The whole Turkish community of the area looked for her but nothing doing. I got the lad's name from Mehmet, checked DVLA and got a registration number and made a couple of calls to people I knew in the Met; we had the car found outside a B&B in Greenwich and the couple inside. I paid them a visit and persuaded the boy he'd rather face Mehmet than me when he refused to take the girl back; amazing what an index finger bent back to the point of breaking from the knuckle can do to change a person's mind. Yes, I know I'm cruel, but come on – the girl was just fourteen; it might be legal in Turkey, but it certainly isn't in the Borough. I took them back and haven't paid for a takeaway since. I would go more often, but I find it embarrassing. I see the daughter around now and again, she always smiles in a friendly way, behind the smile maybe a yearning to plunge a knife in my back; as for the boy I have no idea what happened to him, but the doner kebabs tasted better after that. I joke! I hope.

I picked up the meal, put a tenner on the counter, hurried out before Mehmet could pick it up and catch me and made my way back to the office.

Gold had got the other pages laid out on the desk.

'Some very interesting stuff here.' She picked up a page.

'Wait, food first.' I was starving, and I didn't want bits of kebab and salad on the pages. Eating a doner kebab full to the brim is an art – if you manage without some salad spilling out, you are a kebab pro. I never could, so I made more coffee for us both – coffee and kebabs, a perfect marriage – and we sat away from the desk and enjoyed our meal.

I picked up the wrappers when we'd finished, put them in the trash bin and we both washed our hands.

'Okay, let me tell you what I've found out about our lady.' I told Gold what Mehmet had told me as we dried our hands. 'So we have a name to go on, Serife Aydin, and we know she's a top peg in the Turkish military. I'll get digging on her tomorrow. What have you got from the other papers?'

'Murder, mayhem and financial investments moving around the world – all associated with arms dealing.'

'Sounds interesting.' I settled back to listen.

Gold took a long breath and began. 'Okay, the obituaries are all of top business people: three men and one lady, high flyers in big UK and international companies. Their deaths were all in the last six year period and they were all late middle age or older, so none of the deaths were flagged up as suspicious.' She pointed out the papers one by one. 'Herbert Langford, CEO of First Security, an international company with interests varying from mining in Africa to helicopter gun ship component manufacturing. Julian Hastings, MD of DPL, a London-based small arms manufacturer with government supply contracts worldwide, including the Middle East. Sir Randolph Roberts, owner of Mercandle Enterprises, ammunition suppliers including grenades and air-to-earth missiles; and Estelle Barniere, CEO of Euro Systemes in France, a conglomerate working in the air-space defence area.' She paused and looked up. 'Get the gist?'

'Yes, I don't think any of them would be in the running for the Nobel Peace Prize.'

'Not a chance – all those companies are in the top ten of arms and weapons suppliers worldwide. Anyway, over the six years covering their deaths each of the companies they worked for had their public shares gradually bought up by a shell company in the Caymans called, and you'll love this...'

'Go on?'

'Rambart-Reynolds International.'

It took me a few seconds to get the connection: Nicholas Rambart and my client Jameson Reynolds – the same Jameson Reynolds who told me he didn't know anything about the Rambarts. He was part of the armaments smuggling, and a big part at that. So just what game was he playing?

'You're kidding me?'

'I'm not – that company now has financial control of those companies; and, listen to this, as leading shareholders they replaced the dead executives with people from Rambart-Reynolds International, and over a period of time with their majority share holdings were able to elect more of their people onto the various boards.'

'Sounds like they have a pretty good foothold in the armaments market.'

'If you combine the turnover of those companies, only BASF is bigger in the weapons market.'

'If I was the CEO of BASF I'd be worried.'

'And quite right to be – not all those bosses died in their beds. Julian Hastings fell from the twentieth floor balcony whilst on holiday in Barcelona with a belly full of whisky, and Herbert Langford had a skiing holiday accident – went off piste and down the side of the mountain. Ringing any bells?'

'Eve Rambart's previous husbands.'

'Correct.'

'So she must have been part of the plan at that time.'

'Yes. So who killed her, and why?'

'Got to be Nicholas Rambart – her body was taken to his warehouse, probably to be dropped into a vat of acid or cremated on a bonfire; and after all he's the one who offered a million to me to kill her.'

'Don't you think it strange you haven't heard from him at all?'

I hadn't really thought about it like that; I just thought I'd better keep out of his way for a while after the warehouse break-in and his wife's murder at the apartment. 'Strange in what way?'

'Maybe he's dead – maybe the lady Serife Aydin is knocking them off and the Turks are taking over? They would have lost quite a few millions in the ship going down and God knows how much when their arms warehouse went up. They can't be too happy – that's a lot to replace and a lot of money needed to do it.'

I nodded, 'Cheaper if you own the production companies.'

'Yes, much cheaper, all done at cost.'

'Okay, so if that is the game then there's only one person left to pull the strings at the top.'

'Reynolds.'

'Who is now in mortal danger – or in complete control with Aydin.'

'Are you going to tell Woodward, put him in the picture? Might be a good time to hand it over and back out.'

She was making sense, but I didn't like Reynolds lying to me – I'd been played by him; all that nonsense about only knowing Rambart six months and I shouldn't touch Eve Rambart or Nicholas with a bargepole. But he didn't know she had already told me that it was him who had suggested me to her, so what was he up to? No wonder he had me sweep his office for explosives; if he was a player in this armaments game with the Turks and the IRG, he was walking a thin line. Perhaps Eve Rambart had asked him to recommend a security firm for some task like sweeping for bugs, knowing his past and knowing that anybody he suggested would probably be in the hit market too. No, I wasn't going to hand over to Woodward; I wanted to open the boxes on this one, even if some of those boxes might go bang. First job was to find if Nicholas Rambart was dead or alive – but I would send Woodward the photos of the paperwork and details on Serife Aydin. Just a safety net really; if I ended up dead he'd have the means to follow up the case with MI6's forensic accountants, trace the money, trace the shares, re-open the four CEOs' deaths and put it all together and make arrests.

Life is never straightforward. One minute I'm going to be very rich with a million, maybe two, in the bag, and the next I'm down to two hundred grand and mixed up with MI6, a Turkish lady assassin and a friend who may not be a friend after all. Perhaps I should try being the sort of PI who *follows the wife to find out who's shagging her for the husband*; sounds a much easier way to make a living.

****

CHAPTER 21

Nicholas Rambart had disappeared, but whether he was dead or alive I didn't know – what I did know was that he'd disappeared from his Hilton suite. Alarm bells rang in my head when I went to see if I could get a meet with him in the hotel bar, a very public place; always choose a public place if the person you are meeting might have a reason to kill you – at least I wouldn't be snuffed out there, might get a drive-by as I walk from the hotel, but inside I was pretty safe. The alarm bells rang when I went to ask reception to phone up and tell him I was in the foyer; I had hoped that might bring him down for a chat. He would be surprised I knew where he was for a start and would want to know how I found him, but the first thing I noticed at the reception glancing at his keycard pigeon hole was that the card was there but no green or red slide was showing. The suite was vacant.

'They left yesterday,' was the receptionist's answer to my question.

'Any forwarding address for mail?'

'No sir, sorry.'

I was tempted to drive into the city and face Reynolds with what I knew, see his reaction, but I thought better of it; I had the upper hand knowing he was involved, and he didn't know that I knew that. Complicated, eh?

So that really only left one way forward.

****

We were parked in the darkness sixty metres away from the main gates to the Purley warehouse. The exterior floodlit the entrance and security gatehouse; a single guard sat inside watching TV. I was ready for another look inside: dark clothes, earpiece, Beretta 92 and AK-47, 'tooled up' as some of my criminal friends would call it.

'Are you going in the back way again?' Gold asked.

'No point, go strut your stuff, time to upset the apple cart.'

I couldn't see any reason to take on the razor wire again – this would surely be the end game; we knew what was what and who was who, and just needed to tie up the loose ends and put an end to Rambart and Reynolds's business.

I watched as Gold left the car and made her way towards the gates. When she got to within twenty metres she started wandering a little on her feet; she hadn't told me how she had attracted the guard from the gatehouse the last time we were here, now I guessed she'd played the drunk slapper card – it never fails. It didn't this time either. She got to the gate and the guard hadn't seen her, so she grabbed the gates where the padlock and chain fasten them together and shook them about. That got his attention. He must have recognised her as he was on his way out of the gatehouse and across the driveway pretty quickly – and he was smiling. They exchanged some words; it all seemed very cordial, he was smiling and Gold was laughing.

She reached through with her right hand and patted his arms – it was getting personal, I knew what was coming next; he didn't. Her right hand reached up quickly to behind his head and rammed it forward onto the steel gate bars at speed, knocking him out. The guard slumped to the ground and Gold knelt to unhook his key chain from his belt and quickly found the one that released the chain from the gates. I picked up her AK-47 and joined her as she closed the gate and draped the padlock and chain in position but didn't lock it; a quick escape might be needed. I did a fireman's lift on the guard and carried him back into the gatehouse. Gold joined me. We used a roll of duct tape from the desk to secure his hands behind him and tie his feet together, plus a piece over his mouth and round his head. The cut and bruise on his forehead from his meeting with the steel gate post was pretty savage, so I taped over it to stem the blood – this man was going to have one hell of a headache. Lastly I bent his legs up behind him and taped them to his hands and pushed him under the desk.

Gold had been kneeling at the door, her AK-47 poised.

'All quiet?'I asked.

'All quiet.'

'Follow me.' I led off to the side of the building, thinking the side door that I got through the last time would be our best bet for entry. It was. A triangle of light came out of it and lit the ground; it was open. A car was parked nearby.

'Rambart's car,' Gold whispered.

We kept to the other side of the drive that circled the warehouse keeping close to the perimeter wall – the dark side – and made it to the far side of the car. I pushed a hand over the bonnet; it was warm, a good sign that whoever was inside had recently arrived and hopefully had enough business to do to keep them busy whilst we took a look around.

I clicked the safety off my AK-47 and quickly made it round the car to the door; I listened – no sounds. I peeped inside, couldn't see anybody so I slowly moved inside. It seemed empty, lots of various sized wooden crates just like last time in stacks and singles, somebody could be there amongst them and out of my view. Gold joined me.

'I'll go right, you go left – check it's all clear.' Army training kicking in: you circle right, your partner circles left, that way you cover all the sniper angles.

We met at the far side of the warehouse. I pointed to the steel staircase at the end and the office on the mezzanine floor that held it. 'Cover me.'

She nodded. I made my way through the crates to the staircase and started up them. I could hear talking coming from the office. The blinds were closed so I couldn't see who was inside from the staircase; maybe I would get a peep through at the top.

I didn't get that far. The crack of the shot and the metallic *ting* of the bullet ricocheting off the metal stairs were simultaneous.

'Don't move, stay where you are!' The loud shout came from the open door; I knew who it was by the accent. I was right. Serife Aydin stood just inside the warehouse door holding a pistol with both hands that was pointing my way. A professional grip; aiming a pistol from that distance with one hand and the percentages were in favour of missing the target, with two hands the percentages favoured hitting it. As the target was me I did as I was told and raised my hands as an added reason for her not to shoot; I couldn't see Gold but felt good that she was out there somewhere and would know what was going on. Above me those in the office had heard the shot, the office door banged open and Grant Rankin came out, pistol in hand. He took in the scene and turned the gun on me. He didn't speak; he didn't need to, he could see the situation from above.

Aydin shouted at me, 'Put your weapons on the stair above you.'

I laid my AK-47 where she had said and raised my hands again as she came to the foot of the staircase, a few metres away from me.

'I am not stupid. The gun as well, very slowly.'

It was worth a try. I took out my Beretta 92 slowly and placed it on the stair with the butt towards me so I'd be able to pick it up and fire it in one movement if I got the chance. Yes, I know it's an old model automatic but I still rate it as a top pistol.

'Put your hands behind your head, come down the stairs slowly and sit on the floor.'

That put an end to any thought of grabbing my pistol. I did as I was told.

The office door opened and Nicholas Rambart came out, followed by... Eve Rambart! What the...? I'd seen her shot and carted away in a carpet tube. I kept quiet as Rankin led them down the stairs. Then I noticed Eve Rambart was handcuffed.

'Mr Nevis,' Nicholas smiled at me. 'You really are becoming a pain in the arse. I gave you one job to do and plainly you failed me.' He waved a hand towards his wife. 'She's still alive.'

I took the plunge, hoping to confuse him. 'I saw her shot. I saw her shot in the Knightsbridge apartment.'

Nicholas laughed. 'No, Mr Nevis, you saw her tasered. You saw exactly what we wanted you to see.'

That shook me back a bit. '*Wanted* me to see?'

'Yes, of course. You don't think that your spy nest in the building opposite went unnoticed surely? That nasty incident on the landing with one of Woodward's spooks set our alarm bells ringing; they obviously knew about the apartment and would be watching it – just a matter of finding where from. Didn't take long, but we found *you* watching us from the building opposite, not Woodward. He must have picked us up on one of his many street cameras masquerading as a traffic sensor.'

'Why would you taser your wife?'

'I wanted you to believe she was dead – after all, you had a million pound contract on her life; you might have carried it out and that would have been very unfortunate.'

'Unfortunate how?'

'Well, things had come to light that changed the situation. If you remember our meeting, I told you I didn't want to become the third of her husbands to die suspiciously.'

I nodded.

'Mr Nevis, in my business you deal in very big amounts of money; you create relationships with people who are, shall we say, open to other offers as the merchandise we offer is not always available on the open market.'

'Banned by the Geneva Arms Convention,' I said.

He shrugged. 'Well, in a way yes, some products are made and available but only to certain countries. Other countries we are not permitted to sell them to, and of course that ...' His voice tailed off as he hunched his shoulders and spread his palms.

I finished his sentence, 'Creates a black market.'

He smiled, 'A very lucrative black market.' He turned to Eve. 'My dear wife here has been, unknown to me, a very big player in that black market. A very big player for a considerable time on behalf of the IRG, using me – just as she had used her previous husbands – to provide arms to them, which is why she is still alive. She is a bargaining chip, Mr Nevis, she is not what she seems, she is an agent in the Defence Procurement Department of the Iranian Government – not even Woodward knows that. Iran will want her back and will do a very good prisoner exchange to get her – that is why she is still alive.'

I was confused. 'But those crates went to Turkey, not Iran.'

'Turkey is a staging post. In my business one keeps a very low profile, as you know – you could only find one picture of me, and a very out-of-date one at that. I keep everything at arm's length – double arm's length if I can – and this warehouse is a case in point. Yes, it is rented to a subsidiary company of my businesses but I had never been here until a few weeks ago. One of my trusted managers had noted that we had more crates than we should have had; a week later he disappears. Strange, eh? To cut a long story short, Mr Nevis, my dear wife, who handles my accounts, had ordered more of certain products than I needed to fulfil my genuine orders, and these *extras* were on a separate invoice which was paid for by bank transfer of funds from Switzerland – exactly the same as the way I make payments, so nobody thought anything was strange.' He took a deep breath. 'But those funds came from an IRG Swiss account, not mine and of course the *extras* ordered were for the IRG. Clever, eh?'

'Very.'

'And so the crates were shipped out with my genuine crates to my genuine customer, the Turkish Defence Force, and to their warehouse in Antakya.'

'And they didn't notice?'

'Why would they? A lorry with crates of armaments arrives at an arms store – a perfect ploy. Then those for the IRG are moved on at a later date by IRG people who have infiltrated the warehouse workforce and use false movement paperwork. The military bosses at the warehouse see paperwork that says the arms and missiles are going to their own forward units at the Turkish borders. Everything was working so well for this bitch!' He turned quickly and slapped Eve across the face. She staggered back and fell to the floor. I tensed myself, ready to go for my gun if Gold took this opportunity to open fire. She didn't.

Rambart turned back to me, smiling again. 'And then we had the little episode of the freighter and the Turkish warehouse explosions. Were you responsible for those, Mr Nevis?'

I pursed my lips and shook my head, *no.*

'I am not sure I believe you, anyway it gave the IRG game away. Turkey is a very up-to-date country, Mr Nevis; their forensic scientists are second to none, and it quickly became clear that an explosion of that magnitude was far too big for what should have been in that warehouse at the time, and the remnants of missiles and arms that they pieced together afterwards far outnumbered the official listings of what should be there.' He paused for effect. 'So that was when my dear friend Serife Aydin, my long time contact and Commander in the Turkish Special Forces, took control.' He gave a small bow in her direction. 'As luck would have it, she is a remarkable likeness to my wife. Just a few tweaks to the hairstyle and she could fool anybody from a distance – even you.' Things were falling into place; I was beginning to understand the whole scenario. Eve Rambart was an IRG agent. She had married the bosses of the biggest arms producing companies, murdered them and taken control of the companies making sure of a continuing supply to Iran through the Turkey warehouse scam.

A car pulled up outside. I noticed that Aydin never took her eye or the gun off me. A car door shut and Jameson Reynolds came in. He stood for a moment and took in the situation.

'I wondered why the gate wasn't locked and no security at the front.' He walked over and stood beside Aydin. 'Hello Ben, looks like you've got yourself in a bit of a mess.'

'I should have known you'd be involved.'

'Money, Ben, you know how I get attracted to it – the more the better. My good friend Nicholas was dealing above his financial limit, and with his business being a little, shall we say, under the radar, normal lines of credit were closed to him.'

'You always were the money man.'

'Minimum risk, Ben – stay in the background, hands off and charge a good rate of interest. There's always somebody who needs a loan and if they default, well, there's always people like you and Grant to persuade them not to.' He looked up at Rankin. So that's Rankin's role: enforcer.

Was that what had happened: Rambart hadn't made payments to Reynolds that were due, so he took part of his business? I knew from the old gangster days Reynolds never ever let anybody default – never. Another piece of jigsaw fell into place.

Reynolds pulled a pair of latex gloves from his coat pocket, pulled them on and then walked over and reached through the stair rail and picked up my gun. 'Unfortunately, once in a while somebody doesn't tell me the truth as to who they are and who they are doing business with. I don't like that, especially when the promised payment isn't made on time. But of course you know that Ben, don't you – you must remember a few payment overdue *reminders* you gave to people for me in the old days? Of course you do – and also the final chapter if nothing happened, examples had to be made. Just as now, an example has to be made.'

The fear on Nicholas Rambart's face turned to shock as Reynolds pointed the gun and shot Eve Rambart in the head. He walked over to where she had fallen and made sure she was dead with another shot.

He turned to me. 'That was your job, Ben. Nicholas offered you a million to do that, same as Eve offered you a million to kill Nicholas. I told you I'd recommended them both to you. I knew what they wanted, of course I did, and you could have done it, just like the old days when you got rid of a couple of people for me – easy money Ben, if you'd done it.'

Another piece fell into place, 'Leaving you in sole charge of Rambart- Reynolds International.'

He looked surprised. 'My word Ben, you have done your homework haven't you. Yes, correct, I would have been the major shareholder and CEO of a company with the sole rights to sell arms, both legal and illegal, to Turkey, one of the biggest arms buyers in the world and my dear friend here, Commander Aydin would see that it stayed that way without the likes of Eve Rambart using it for getting illegal arms to her Iranian masters. But you didn't do the job, did you Ben, so I have to complete it.'

He raised the gun and shot Nicholas Rambart in the head; Nicholas Rambart slumped to the floor like a rag doll. Reynolds turned back to me. I knew that if he lifted the gun towards me Gold would take him out.

'Nicholas was a fool Ben, he had no idea what was going on right under his own eyes until I told him. Eve was very good at her job. She fooled me at the beginning as we took over the four biggest ordnance manufacturers one by one, I thought it was just business, no idea she was putting it all together for the IRG. I was a partner with her from the beginning, the plan worked well, she married the bosses and I arranged their *accidental* deaths once they had changed their wills so that she inherited their major share holdings and control of the companies. She was good, so bloody good even I didn't realise she was shipping extras destined for Iran. When I found out I played the pair of them against each other and it has worked out just as I thought it would.' He looked down at Nicholas Rambart's still body, 'I do believe I am now the major shareholder and CEO of the company – perhaps I should change its name from Rambart-Reynolds International to just Reynolds International, eh?' He smiled and pointed at the bodies, 'Two dead Ben – killed by your gun with your bullets in their heads, professional job. The sort of hit the police know you are capable of; the sort of hit they know you have done in the past and never nailed you for, so a feather in their caps to have you in the frame with such strong evidence on these two killings, eh? Have you guessed the plan yet?'

I hadn't. But I knew Gold wouldn't let too much harm come my way.

Reynolds put my gun on the floor between the bodies. 'I am going now, Ben – so is Serife. Her bosses will be very pleased that the people organising armament supplies to their enemies in the IRG have been eliminated and business can get back to normal. The only thing that remains is what to do with you? Pretty obvious really Ben, Rankin will kill you – your gun will be in your dead hand and the gun that Rankin kills you with will be in Nicholas's hand. You killed each other. Perhaps you had Eve as prisoner and Nicholas, the dutiful husband, came to rescue her. Who cares? You're both dead and the fingerprints and guns tell whatever story the police like to settle on. Goodbye, Ben. Pity it didn't work out – I quite like you.'

He walked to the door and Aydin went out with him. I looked up at Rankin; I knew Gold would have him in her sights and if he pointed his gun at me he was dead.

He didn't point his gun at me; he came down a few stairs with it held at his side pointing at the floor and slowly and purposely he moved his arm out to the right, pointing the gun towards the wooden crates on the right-hand side of the warehouse. He loosed off a shot waited a few seconds and fired another one then slowly bent and put his gun on the stairs before raising his arms and coming down. When he was a few stairs away from his gun I moved fast and picked mine up and covered him. He kept coming down and stopped at the bottom.

'What are you playing at, Rankin?'

'Reynolds would have heard those shots Ben, he'll think I killed you, one to the body and one to the head. Tell your partner she can come out now.'

I didn't need to; Gold emerged from between two stacks of crates on my right, her AK-47 up and pointing at Rankin.

He smiled. 'Did Woodward give you a phone?'

'Yes.'

'Got it with you?'

'Yes.'

'Take a picture of me and send it.'

'Why?'

'You'll see why. Do it please.'

I took Woodward's mobile from my trouser thigh pocket, switched it on, took a picture of Rankin standing with his hands in the air and sent it. Almost immediately it rang.

'Yes.'

Woodward's voice was very calm. 'He's one of ours.'

'He could have been killed.'

'What is happening?'

I explained where we were and what had unfolded.

'Put Rankin on.'

I passed the phone over. Rankin listened for quite a while before closing it and passing it back.

'There's a team of cleaners coming over to clear all this up and get rid of the bodies. Once that's done the Anti Terrorism Boys will come in and remove any paperwork from the office, then the Army Ordnance will clear the warehouse. I'm to stay and supervise. Nothing happened here, Ben – the warehouse will become vacant.'

'And us?' I shifted my hand between Gold and me.

'You've forty-eight hours before the fraud squad go into Rambart- Reynolds International with warrants and the Stock Exchange delists it.'

'Forty-eight hours to do what?'

'Woodward didn't say.' Rankin smiled and shrugged. 'But I personally wouldn't be too happy about being played like that by Reynolds, if you see what I mean. Nasty piece of work – we could do without people like that.'

Well, if that wasn't a nod and a wink I don't know what is.

'And the Turkish Army lady?'

'Foreign Office will raise a deportation order on her, but she'll probably be on her way to catch a flight to Turkey as we speak. If she isn't then I would guess that as soon as the balloon bursts at Rambart-Reynolds she will be.' He held his hand out and we shook. 'Good to work with you again Ben, even though you didn't know we were.' He turned to Gold and shook her hand too. 'Thank you for not being trigger-happy,'

We walked towards the door, then a thought struck me and I shouted back. 'Oh, I forgot – there's a security guard under the desk in the gatehouse that might need some medical treatment.'

****

CHAPTER 22

I didn't sleep well. Every time I thought of Reynolds I got angry; I'd done him lots of favours in the distant past, lots. I'd taken people off his back, nasty people, and even sent a couple to the magician – the magician being a chap I know who makes things disappear, mainly bodies. Okay, so Reynolds had put me in line for a couple of million quid, but only to harvest multi-millions for himself and then kill me afterwards. Yes, I was angry. I finally got to sleep about four in the morning and didn't wake 'til after midday. I showered and ate a bowl of All-Bran sprinkled with walnuts, my regular breakfast – keeps the bowels moving, and if that part of your system is working regular everything else will be too. I gave Gold a call.

'You okay?'

'Fine, you?'

'Yes, still bloody angry at Reynolds.'

She paused for a moment. 'Have you forgotten something?'

'It's not your birthday again, is it?' Four years running I'd missed her birthday; it's on my mobile with an alarm flag, but I hadn't heard it beep.

'No, not my birthday.'

'Okay so what have I forgotten?' I was expecting some mundane trivial thing.

'You've got a set of keys to Reynolds's dealing rooms.'

Of course I had – of bloody course I had. I used them to go in with the sweep team every month after office hours. How could I forget that?

'He won't be expecting you – you're dead.'

'I am, aren't I.' I thought for a couple of moments. 'Are you gold-digging tonight?'

'No.'

'Okay, meet you in the car park here at midnight.'

'Okay.' She rang off.

I had some work to do.

****

Gilbert Charles, not his real name, owns an up-market gunsmith's in St Martin's Lane, just up from Trafalgar Square. The old-fashioned brass hanging doorbell rang when I went in. Charles was fiddling about at the counter polishing a shotgun; his main income came from the country set, the toffs who bred birds in order to kill them in their first year of life – nice people. I once dreamt about having a line of them running off over a gorse scrub whilst I pumped lead into their arses from a double-barrel. I get dreams like that; never forgotten that one. I ought to get help really.

'Mr Nevis, long time no see.' Gilbert put down the gun and shook my hand, his welcome genuine. He gave every impression of being a country gent himself: tweed check jacket, cavalry twill trousers, brown brogues – all he needed was a deerstalker hat to complete the image.

'How are you, Gilbert – still facilitating the deaths of a million birds every year?' I read the word *facilitating* in the paper a couple of weeks ago and had been itching to use it ever since. Silly, eh?

Gilbert spread his hands and made like Fagin. 'Got to make a penny or two.'

We go back quite a way do Gilbert and me; if his la-di-da clients knew his background they'd run a mile. His main income, before he served seven years for it, was refurbishing collectors' vintage guns so they could shoot again, and selling or renting to the criminals who used them on robberies or worse. The top twelve inches from the barrels of double-barrelled shotguns were often removed in Gilbert's workshop to produce a handy sawn-off version that would probably be pushed into the face of some petrified bank or post office employee. A leopard doesn't change its spots, so I had no doubt Gilbert was still active in that business behind the facade of his posh shop.

I had written down what I wanted; people like Gilbert are always under some sort of surveillance. The Organised Crime Squad know as well as I do that Gilbert's skills are more in demand today than ever before, and will often slip a hidden microphone into premises in the dead of night. I've done it myself. So you never know who's listening.

Gilbert took the list I passed over and read it. 'I think we can accommodate you, sir,' he said with a big smile. 'Please take a seat whilst I check the stock room.' He pointed to a pair of fake antique chairs at the back of the shop. I sat down on one and he disappeared into the back room, returning five minutes later carrying a shoebox-size box printed with his fake Gilbert Charles family monogram which he slid into a 'Gilbert Charles Country Sports' bag and handed to me over the counter. 'I'm happy to say we had your requirements in stock, sir.'

I pulled out a small wad of twenty pound notes, five hundred pounds total. Gilbert counted out three hundred and gave me back the rest. 'I'll put it on your account, sir,' he said loudly; he'd cottoned on to my reservations about a bug. 'Thank you so much, I do hope you find everything satisfactory.'

We smiled at each other and I left the shop.

****

Gold was already there when I took the service lift down to the car park at midnight carrying Gilbert's box. She slipped out of her Lexus and into my Honda CRV. She was in dark mode, black jeans and sweater – so was I. She carried her Burberry shoulder bag; no doubt it held a variety of tools we might need.

Twenty minutes later we were parked in a dark back alley beside the city office block where Reynolds's dealing room took up all the top floor. The whole building was in darkness. I knew there was no night security – strange really seeing that most of the offices in the block were company dealing rooms and full of computers and IT hard and soft ware, all very much in demand in both the honest and not so honest secondhand market. One raid with a large van and a dodgy trader could keep himself going on eBay for a year.

Gold rummaged in her Burberry and gave me a head torch, earpiece and clip-on microphone. She would stay put and keep watch for any security patrols whilst I was inside; the City of London streets can be very busy at night with security companies doing their rounds, and if any of the other tenants of Reynolds's building had a contract with one I didn't want to bump into them inside.

Entering was easy; on my first visit to do a bug sweep Reynolds had given me the keypad numbers to the staff side door. I took the stairs up, my Gilbert Charles monogrammed box under my arm; lifts make a noise and maybe somebody was working late in one of the other floor's dealing rooms playing the markets in a different time zone – you can't be too careful.

When I got to the top floor I checked carefully through the double glass door just in case; it was empty, all in darkness – no computers flashing stock movements and currency trades; their screens were asleep, their pixels waiting for the surge of electricity that would wake them up for another day of frenetic work. It was a large open plan room the size of a tennis court arranged in four long rows of joined desks; each had computers and plasma screens of all sizes stacked on them with banks of telephones sitting in front. Reynolds's glass office was positioned off the back of it, set a couple of feet above the dealing floor level with three wide steps up to it. He could see everybody was working hard from his desk in there.

I used my key, went inside and stood for a moment, sizing up my options. The suspended ceiling was a favourite; I knew from working on the security sweeps that the light polystyrene tiles slid out of their metal frames easily to give access to the original roof above. The cavity between was about four feet high. I opened the Gilbert Charles box on the nearest desk to me and took out a dozen split second LED timers, then very carefully pulled out a block of C4 plastic explosive. I like C4 as you can mould it and chuck it about a bit without it exploding – it needs an electric charge sent through it to set it off; it's the demolition man's choice of weapon. I pulled off pieces and rolled them into twelve six-inch sausages, then putting them and the timers back in the box I walked through the dealing room and into Reynolds's office. Standing on his large desk shifted a ceiling tile aside. I set a timer for 7.10 a.m., pushed it into a C4 sausage which I wrapped around one of the metal ties that strung the suspended ceiling framework up to the original concrete ceiling and roof above it and then put the tile back in place. I repeated the operation another eleven times in the dealing room moving along on top of a row of desks, one sausage with timer above every sixth tile in a row towards the double entrance doors, each timer set ten seconds after the one before. This was going to be one hell of a firework display! The amount of C4 wouldn't bring the building down, but there wouldn't be much of Reynolds's dealing room or computers left standing after they'd gone off, and with a bit of luck not much of him left either. I had set the first one to go off at 7.10a.m. as I knew Reynolds got in his office at 6.30a.m., and his staff arrived at 8a.m. – I just hoped nobody had decided to make an early start.

I left the floor and started down the staff stairs when Gold came through on the earpiece.

'Company.'

I froze. 'Go on?'

'Cleaners, two of – coming up from the staff entrance.'

I could hear them now – foreign voices, and they were coming up the stairs, why hadn't they taken the lift! I retraced my steps up to the top floor, listening and hoping they'd move off the staircase into an office below; they didn't. I let myself back into Reynolds's floor – surely he hadn't hired night cleaners? As far as I remembered he had a company come in every day at close of business at about five o'clock and do a clean. I checked the waste bins nearest to me – full of shredded paper, a bad sign; he must have changed things. I hit the fluorescent light switches and the floor was bathed in a white light. I sat at a desk halfway down the aisle and hit all the hardware switches; screens flickered into action and the pixels danced, showing graphs and bars and flashing red and green stock prices from God knows where in the world at that time of night.

The two cleaners came in and stopped, surprised the lights were on and even more surprised that some fool was working at this time of night. I gave them a friendly wave and smile; they nodded back.

'Just finishing up,' I shouted.

One of them smiled and laughed. 'We can go – can come back later.'

'No, no, I'm off now,' I replied.

He translated to his friend and they started emptying the waste bins into plastic refuse sacks. I switched off the hardware and made towards the door. 'Have a good night,' I shouted.

They both nodded and I left the floor, took the stairs two at a time and rejoined Gold.

'Hungry?' I asked her. I was.

'I wouldn't say no to a rib-eye steak, salad and chips.'

Ten minutes late we stood beside an all night burger van on the Embankment off Battersea Bridge, chomping through cheeseburgers washed down with some of the best coffee you can get in London.

'You really know how to impress a lady don't you, eh?' Gold said between mouthfuls.

Well, it was either that or a jellied eel and whelk stall down the Commercial Road. Some people are never satisfied.

****

CHAPTER 23

Jameson Reynolds felt good. There was a definite spring in his step and a smile across his face as he walked through the dealing room and sat in his office, putting his Costa coffee on the desk in front of him. He didn't know why he stopped at the coffee shop every day on his way in for a take-out of the tasteless drink at three quid a cup when there was always plenty of decent coffee pods and milk in the dealing room where he had three Barista coffee machines for the staff to help themselves; but the other city high-flyers seemed to do it, so he did. Good for the image was how he viewed it. His smile broke into laughter as he flipped off the lid and took a sip. He raised the cup as though toasting a deal.

'Here's to you, Ben – so predictable and so gullible. Shame to lose you, but that's life. Winner takes all.'

He switched on his screens and checked the Reynold-Rambart stock price. He was the major shareholder and would have his dealers buy as much as they could before announcing Rambart's *retirement* and his own elevation to chairman – his people on the board would nod that through. He had checked the papers and the BBC News website both days since the warehouse episode to see if there was any mention of it; there wasn't. The Foreign Office was probably keeping it quiet with a DSMA-Notice whilst they cleared things up. They wouldn't want a spat with Iran if they could avoid it. '*Well done, Rankin. I wonder what you did with Nevis's body? Not that I particularly care.*' He checked his watch; it was coming up to ten past seven. The daily papers should have been left in the building foyer by now; he read them all closely every day, looking for any indication of something happening to companies of countries that could move a share or currency market – early bird gets the worm. He stood and stretched, took another sip of coffee and walked out of his office.

The explosion behind him startled him and shook him rigid as he turned and saw the ceiling crashing down, covering his desk with burning ceiling tiles, plaster, twisted metal frames and concrete. The desk he had been sitting at moments before. He made for the main door where a row of powder fire extinguishers stood, but in front and above him the ceiling exploded again bringing him to standstill; he covered his face with his arm and started running towards the doors but he was running under a storm of crashing ceiling, twisted metal and broken concrete. The roof was straining against the explosions that were ripping it apart above and in front of him as he ran showering him with bricks and concrete, until the debris on the floor piled up blocking his path and the constant hammering of falling broken concrete falling on him sent him half unconscious to the floor a few feet from the doors. Computers and screens were toppling as the rows of desks gave way under the weight of the debris landing on them and Jameson Reynolds was becoming buried. He lifted his head, wiping blood from his eyes, and the only thing he could see as the debris piled on top of him was a battered shoebox-sized box with the Gilbert Charles coat of arms printed on it. He knew Gilbert Charles from his organised crime days and of course he knew the one person who would use him. The last thing Jameson Reynolds said before the rest of the roof came down and crushed the life out of him was: 'Nevis, you bastard.'

THE END

Other Ben Nevis & The Gold Digger books

Book 2. **The National Treasure.**
The daughter of a respected stage actress a *national treasure* disappears. Drugs, Romanian crime gangs and people who aren't what they appear to be emerge from the shadows. Can Ben and Gold get the girl back? Is the '*national treasure'* maybe a little bit tarnished?

****

Book 3. **Chinese Takeaway.**
GCHQ is missing a code box. The codes control the UK missile defence satellite system. Chasing the box through Madeira and Morocco puts Ben and Gold in direct conflict with the Chinese and Moroccan Secret Service and they don't take prisoners. Then there is the UK Minister unexpectedly turning up and a double agent in MI6. The body count rises as the pace increases.

****

Book 4. **Double Trouble**
Nuclear scientists are being kidnapped from Porton Down by the Russian Secret Service and taken to a unit in Belarus to work on their Thermobaric missile programme. MI6 hire Ben and Gold to bring back the last scientist and destroy the programme. But what if the scientist doesn't want to return? A contemporary

espionage thriller with an explosive ending at the London Russian Embassy.

Check out Barry Faulkner's other crime books here...

www.barry-faulkner.com

DCS Palmer books

Future Riches
The Felt Tip Murders
A Killer is Calling
Poetic Justice
Loot
I'm With The Band
Burning Ambition
Take Away Terror
Ministry of Death
The Bodybuilder
Succession
The Black Rose
Laptops Can Kill
Screen 4

London Crime 1930s-2021 (factual)
UK Serial Killers (factual)

Bidder Beware (Comedy crime)

Printed in Great Britain
by Amazon

56068415R00126